The AMAZING DAYS of ABBY HAYES

Look Before You Leap

Read more books about me!

The AMAZING DAYS of ABBY HAYES

Look Before You Leap

ANNE MAZER

AN
APPLE
PAPERBACK

SCHOLASTIC INC.
New York Toronto London Auckland Sydney
Mexico City New Delhi Hong Kong Buenos Aires

For Mom and Dad

Cover and interior illustrations by Monica Gesue
Book design by Dawn Adelman

ISBN 0-439-34124-8

12 11 10 9 8 7 6 5 4 3 2   2 3 4 5 6 7/0

Printed in the U.S.A   40

First Scholastic Book Club printing, March 2002

Chapter 1

Saturday

"Those who play with cats must expect to get scratched."

—Miguel de Cervantes

Windmill Calendar

Oh, yeah? Marshmallow is a loving, friendly cat who never scratches! She belongs to my neighbor, Heather, who is a graduate student at the university.

Marshmallow has many talents. She holds the world record for the 18-foot dash from couch to food dish. Famous escape artists study her techniques for disappearing out the front door in the blink of an eye. No other cat can run as fast as Marshmallow! She can outrun a locomotive, a speeding bullet, and a fifth-grader in hot (or cold) pursuit!

(And she _never_ scratches!)

Marshmallow has given birth to kittens. Hooray! Hooray! _Hooray!_

Her proud owner, Heather, invited Abby Hayes to her apartment to visit the kittens. "Los gatitos," she called them. "It means little cats in Spanish."

There are seven of the tiny creatures. Three of them are orange striped, two are gray, one is black, and one is white. Did they consult with each other before they were born and decide to wear different outfits?

The new mother now shows no interest in breaking feline speed records or escaping from Heather's apartment. She lies on a pillow, cleaning and feeding her babies. If a kitten wanders too far, Marshmallow picks it up by the scruff of its neck and brings it back. The kittens are small enough to put in a pocket!

Even though they're only a week old,

Marshmallow's kittens have already begun breaking records of their own! Abby plans to give them a page in the <u>Hayes Book of World Records</u> for "Wobbliest Walk and Squeakiest Meow."

Marshmallow's kittens will be friendly like their mother. Maybe they'll be supersonic runners, too!

<u>Abby Hayes wants a pet!!</u>

A kitten would be nice, but she's not fussy. She would be happy with a dog, a fish, a bird, an alligator (ha-ha, just kidding), a boa constrictor (kidding again), or a guinea pig. As long as it's hers to love and take care of!

Abby tightened the strap of her swim goggles and pulled them on. She slipped off her sandals and walked to the deep end of the town pool.

For a moment, she surveyed the pool. The shallow end was crowded with splashing bodies. The deep end was almost empty. Abby tugged at a corner of her new purple bathing suit. Then she took a breath, pinched her nose, and jumped.

With a splash, she landed in the water.

Her best friend, Jessica, swam over to greet her. Jessica's long, straight brown hair was wet and plastered against her head. Her bathing suit had turquoise and white stripes.

"Abby!" she cried. "I earned seven dollars today!"

"Congratulations!" Abby said, treading water.

Jessica had just been hired as a mother's helper. Every weekday morning she played with a four-year-old boy while his mom worked at home.

"How did it go?" Abby asked.

"He threw cereal on me," Jessica said. "Cream of wheat — with maple syrup. I had to give him a time-out."

"Yuk," Abby said. She was glad she didn't have a job. Anyway, she didn't need one. A few months ago, she had held a garage sale and earned $165.00. Even after buying new Rollerblades and pads as well as gifts for her friends and family, Abby still had plenty of spending money left over.

She wished that Jessica had lots of money, too. Then she wouldn't be working as a mother's helper. She'd attend camp with Abby, instead. Every year since kindergarten, Jessica and Abby had gone to summer day camp together. This was the first year that they'd be apart.

Camp wouldn't be the same without Jessica. No close friend to laugh with or to share secrets with in the middle of the day. No one to be her buddy on wilderness hikes. The summer stretched ahead of her, long and a little lonely. Would a pet make it better? Abby couldn't bring a pet to camp, of course. But she wanted someone to play with when she came home.

Jessica dove underwater, then popped up to the surface again. "Maple syrup glues your hair," she told Abby. "I had to shampoo it twice when I got home. It's not safe to have long hair around Geoffrey. Do you think I should cut it off? Before he does?"

"No!" Abby floated on her back. "Just put it up."

Jessica nodded. "I wonder what he'll try next."

The two girls swam across the pool.

"Guess what, Jessica? I'm going to get a pet," Abby announced as they reached the other side.

"Are you allowed? What about your brother's allergies?" Jessica asked. She was well acquainted with allergies. She had asthma and carried an inhaler everywhere. Except in the pool, of course.

"There are pets that don't shed," Abby said, pushing a lock of wet hair from her face. She loved her hair when it was wet: straight, dark, normal hair — not her everyday wild, red, crazy curls. If she didn't brush it, though, it curled even more wildly when it dried.

"Which ones?" her friend asked.

"I don't know yet." She hadn't solved that problem. But why should Alex's allergies stop her? It was simply a matter of research and the proper care.

"Yes, but . . ." Jessica began, when Abby interrupted her.

"Look!" She pointed to the diving board.

While they were talking, a half-dozen kids had lined up in front of the board. Abby and Jessica knew many of them from school.

Mason stood at the front. His stomach ballooned over his bright orange trunks. With a loud snort, he stepped onto the diving board and surveyed the pool.

"Dive already!" It was Zach. His hair was cut to a short stubble and he wore baggy swim trunks that had a pattern of electronic keyboards on them. His arms and legs were skinny and tanned.

"Give someone else a chance!" Tyler echoed. For the summer, he had shaved his head and bleached what was left to a white-blond. Now he and Zach, his best friend, looked almost like twins.

The diving board trembled as Mason strode to the end. He jumped up and down. The board quivered under his weight.

He let out a wild holler, leaped into the air, spread his arms like airplane wings, and hit the water with a tremendous splash.

"Tidal waves!" Zach cried.

Mason emerged, punching the air. "Did you see that? Wasn't it awesome?" He burped loudly.

"You were great!" Tyler yelled.

"I can dive better than that." It was Bethany, best friend of Brianna and resident fifth-grade hamster-lover. She flipped her long blond hair over her shoulder. Everyone made way for her to go up the ladder.

"Where's Brianna?" Abby whispered to Jessica.

Jessica shrugged. "Brianna? She's probably winning awards. Or appearing in commercials, or dancing on Broadway."

Brianna was the champion fifth-grade boaster. She was better at everything than everyone. And Bethany was her personal cheerleader.

At the end of the diving board, Bethany stood very straight and still. Her toes pointed out like a gymnast's. She wore a black bathing suit with a tiny diamond pattern.

"Knock yourself out!" Mason cried. "No one beats the Mason Man!"

Bethany didn't reply. She took a breath, jumped high in the air, somersaulted twice, and entered the water with barely a ripple.

"Hooray!" yelled Abby and Jessica.

As Bethany swam to the surface, everyone applauded her, even the boys.

Mason scowled. "That was a fluke."

"Oh, yeah?" Bethany retorted.

He smacked the water with his hand and burped again. "*Yeah!*"

"Bethany can dive better in her sleep than you!" Abby yelled. "Mason Man!"

With a grateful nod in Abby's direction, Bethany headed toward the ladder. She climbed out of the pool and stood in line at the diving board again.

Mason followed her. "We'll see about that," he growled.

"Let's have a contest!" Natalie cried. She was one of Abby and Jessica's closest friends. Her short dark hair was rumpled and messy. She wore a halter-top bathing suit that was mysteriously free from stains. (Her clothes almost always showed the results of the chemistry experiments she liked to do.)

"A contest! A contest!" Tyler cried.

"What's the prize?" Mason demanded.

"A Swimmer's Calendar!" Abby called out.

"I have eighty-one calendars in my room," she whispered to Jessica. "There's got to be a Swimmer's Calendar *somewhere*."

Calendars lined the walls of Abby's room, filled her desk drawers, and lay on her floor. She was always adding to her collection, especially during birthdays, holidays, and vacations. Her favorite grandmother, Grandma Emma, often sent her calendars for no reason at all.

"What else?" Mason folded his arms over his chest.

"I can give you a free cheat code for an electronic game," Zach offered.

". . . *and* a poster of the space shuttle," Jessica finished.

"I accept!" Bethany said.

"I do, too!" Mason said. "Even though the prizes are crummy. Doesn't anyone want to offer me cash?"

"No!" Jessica and Abby and Tyler and Zach said in unison.

Bethany smoothed an invisible wrinkle from her bathing suit. "I'm ready for the contest. Are you?"

"We need time to practice," Zach said. He darted a quick look at Mason. "How about two months from now?"

"No way!" Abby cried. "That's the end of the summer!"

"Okay, four weeks. Or three," Zach amended.

Mason nodded in agreement.

Like a magician, Natalie waved her hand over the pool. "The contest will be in three weeks," she announced. "Then we'll see who's the best diver in fifth grade."

Chapter 2

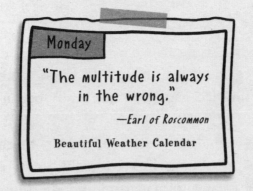

Monday

"The multitude is always in the wrong."

—Earl of Roscommon

Beautiful Weather Calendar

I asked SuperSis Isabel (the human dictionary) what a multitude was. She told me that it was a crowd or a large number of people.

Is the multitude _always_ wrong?

1. There was a multitude of kids at the town pool this weekend. The multitude thinks Bethany is going to win the contest. All the girls and some of the boys are cheering her on.

Bethany is a great diver. Mason isn't. How can we, the multitude, be wrong?

2. If a multitude of Hayes family members wants a pet, then we will get one. Will we be in the wrong? NO!

The Hayes family sat around the kitchen table. They had just finished eating dinner. Abby began clearing the table.

"That was delicious, Eva," their mother said. "Thanks for cooking dinner tonight."

"Frozen peas and macaroni and cheese out of the box?" Isabel, Eva's anything-but-identical twin, said. "Not exactly gourmet food."

"At least I didn't have to cook it," their father said. He poured himself a cup of coffee. "And neither did you, Isabel."

"I cook tomorrow night," Isabel reminded him. "I'm making fettucine Alfredo." She rolled the "r" for an authentic Italian sound.

"Fettucine Fred?" Eva snickered. She stood up. She was wearing running shorts and a Lycra sports top. "I'm off to the gym," she said. "I have to build up my arm again."

She made a muscle with her right arm. It was smaller and weaker looking than the other. Eva had broken her arm during a basketball game last spring. The cast had just come off.

"Wait a minute, Eva." Her mother waved her back to her seat. "Your father and I want to talk about something."

Abby stacked the remaining dishes on the counter. After dinner, her younger brother, Alex, would load them in the dishwasher.

From the look of him, Alex needed to go in the dishwasher, too. There were macaroni stains on his T-shirt and his hair was tangled and uncombed.

"Mom, I don't want to be late," Eva complained.

Isabel blew on her fingernails, which were long, shiny, and polished silver. "Missing ten minutes of your workout isn't a tragedy, Eva. You'll get your arm back. Don't worry."

"Oh, yeah?" Eva said. "How would you know? You've never broken a bone. I have to get in shape before basketball season next fall. To say nothing of lacrosse and softball . . . "

"Let's not start," their father sighed.

Abby sat down in her chair. The last time her parents had called a family meeting was to assign jobs for a backyard cleanup. She had raked leaves for hours. She hoped they didn't have another home improvement project in mind.

Their mother tucked a stray lock of hair into her bun. She had come straight from her law office and hadn't changed out of her suit.

"Has anyone thought about vacation?" Olivia Hayes stirred a teaspoon of sugar into her coffee. "We have a week at the end of the summer. What do you want to do? Let's take a poll."

Four voices spoke up at once.

"See historical sites!" Isabel said. "Revolutionary War battlefields! Colonial settlements!"

"A bike trip!" Eva cried.

"I want to go to a science and technology museum!" Alex shouted.

"Can we spend time with Grandma Emma?" Abby asked. "And visit a calendar factory?"

There was a moment of silence. Isabel broke it. "What do you want to do, Mom and Dad?" she asked.

"Your mother wants to go antiquing," their father said, "and I want to relax on a beach and do nothing for a week."

The six members of the Hayes family looked at each other in dismay.

"We knew this wasn't going to be easy," their mother said.

"How are we going to pack six vacations into one?" Isabel wailed.

Nobody said anything. There was nothing to say.

"Mom, Dad, can we get a pet?" Abby blurted out. She knew it wasn't good timing. It was the worst timing ever, in fact, but somehow the words just flew out of her mouth.

"A pet?" Her father frowned. "Aren't we having enough trouble deciding on a vacation?"

"I've always wanted a dog," Eva said. "A golden retriever."

"Cats," pronounced Isabel, "are the only pets worth having."

"I want a cage full of white mice," Alex said, "that I can study and put through mazes."

"You're allergic to fur and feathers, Alex," their mother pointed out. "That's why we don't have any pets now."

"But Mom — " Abby began. Didn't her mother know about hypoallergenic pets?

Across from her, Isabel and Eva began arguing about cats and dogs. Actually, they were arguing *like* cats and dogs.

"Can we talk about our vacation?" their mother interrupted.

When no one responded, she threw her hands up.

"It's hopeless," Paul Hayes said to his wife with a laugh. "We'll never make a decision tonight."

"And if we get a pet, can we bring it on vacation?" Abby asked.

"Discussion adjourned until tomorrow," their mother said. "Try to think about everyone else's ideas. We'll discuss them and vote on our favorite."

Olivia Hayes banged her spoon on the table like a gavel, then stood up and put an apron over her work clothes. "Alex? Are you ready to help load the dishwasher?"

"Can I go now?" Eva asked.

Their father nodded. Eva picked up her gym bag and disappeared out the back door.

"Eva forgot about dessert." Isabel looked annoyed. Her twin had had the last word.

"Not to worry. We have ice cream in the freezer," their father said.

"Again?" Isabel folded her napkin into a neat triangle and stood up. "I'm going on the Internet to do some research. I'll print out the results for our discussion tomorrow."

Abby went over to the couch and pulled out her purple journal.

Uh-oh!

Isabel Hayes, age fourteen, will make a formal presentation for the family trip. She will tell us that we can relive history by visiting Civil War and Revolutionary battlefields.

Note: Why do we have to relive history? I want relief from history!

Eva Hayes, also fourteen, will praise healthy outdoor exercise and the teamwork of bike trips.

Note: She will not mention sunburn, sore muscles, and mosquito bites.

Seven-year-old Alex Hayes will try to convince us to study robotics and the first computers.

Note: Everyone will pretend to understand what he is saying.

Mom and Dad will talk about collecting antique furniture and escaping from civilization.

Note: Why do parents always choose boring vacations?

As for Abby Hayes, middle daughter...
I will describe playing with Zipper, Grandma Emma's dog. Everyone will remember how much they love Zipper and how much the Hayes family needs a pet! I will also say how much fun it is to see thousands of shiny new calendars all at once!

Note: Everyone will listen politely. Two minutes after I've finished, my family will be arguing about something else! I will enter my plan in the Hayes Book of World Records as "Most Quickly Forgotten Vacation Idea."

No one ever agrees on anything in the Hayes family! We never have a multitude! Does this mean we are all right all the time?

Even if we are, it doesn't get us any closer to choosing a vacation!

Think positive! Find many reasons for taking Isabel's, Eva's, Alex's, or Mom's and Dad's vacations. Entire family will be impressed and grateful. Sisters, brother, and parents will immediately rush out and find a pet for the family.

Positive Thoughts:

Oh, never mind!!!!

I will get a pet, anyway.

Even if my family doesn't agree, I will do it on my own. I don't need their help! I can find a pet and bring it home. I will feed it and play with it. It will be mine, mine, mine! I will take care of it without any help from <u>anyone</u>!

Chapter 3

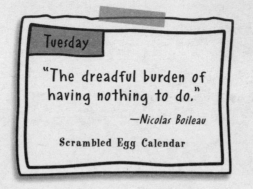

Tuesday

"The dreadful burden of having nothing to do."

—Nicolas Boileau

Scrambled Egg Calendar

I have both too much AND too little to do! That is a really dreadful burden.

There is too little to do with my friends this summer and too much to do with my family!

As Mom said last night, "The ideal Hayes family vacation would be educational, athletic, sociable, and relaxing all at once."

Everyone agreed that sounded awful! No one can do everything at once, can they?

The Hayes family has had four "discussions" already. In spite of this, we are not any closer to deciding on a family trip. We have "agreed to disagree," as Dad said. Why can't we disagree to agree instead?

Mom says we have to reach a consensus. That sounds like a government form to fill out. It really means we need to make a decision. Soon!

SuperSib Isabel announced that we aren't moving forward. "We are stalled," she said.

Isn't stalled what happens to a horse? What next? Will the Hayes family start eating hay?

Typical Vacation Conversation
Someone: "What about—?"
Someone else: "No!"
Someone: "But..."
Someone else: "NO!"
Someone: "What if—?"
Someone else: "ABSOLUTELY NOT!"

If this keeps up, the Hayes family will need an Argument Vacation.

(I bet we'd argue over that, too!)

CHANGE OF SUBJECT!!!! (Before I start arguing with _myself_!)

Abby's Ideal Summer Schedule

7:00 a.m. Wake up. (Helped by alarm clock and loud chirping birds outside window.)

7:03 a.m. Write in journal. (Very important. Equal to food, water, and medicine.)

7:25 p.m. Play with pet.

7:55 a.m. Dad knocks on door and tells me breakfast is ready.

8:03 a.m. Eat breakfast with Alex.

8:30 a.m. Camp. Hiking, boating, arts and crafts. Best friends are all there. We do everything together.

2:30 p.m. Camp over.

2:45 p.m. Put on bathing suit. Pack bag with towel, goggles, sandals, and snacks.

3:00 p.m. At pool. All friends are there. Swim, snack, and dive until 7:00 p.m.

7:00 p.m. Home for dinner. Play with pet again.

<u>Abby's Actual Summer Schedule</u>

The same as above, except I don't have a pet or <u>any</u> friends at camp. The program starts next week.

<u>How to Get Pet, Part 1</u>:

a. Go to pet camp. (Is there such a thing?) Spend the week with every kind of pet, and at the end of the session, take one home. Feed lettuce to a bunny with a twitching pink nose, toss sticks to a dog in a field, and teach a parrot to say, "I want pierced ears."

<u>That</u> would impress my parents! They'd give me permission to get pierced ears right away!

b. Walk Mrs. Odell's dogs with Jessica. (Maybe Mrs. Odell has an extra to give me? Or knows of puppies that need a loving home?)

c. Don't forget to call Jessica first!

(She said yes! I can walk the dogs with her this evening.)

<u>Dog-walking Report</u> (from your canine re-porter, Abby Hayes)

The Dogs:

The dogs' names are Elvis, Buddy, and Prince.
Elvis is small, white, and furry.
Prince is large, golden, and friendly.
Buddy is short, brown, and stubby.

General Dog Behavior:

Number of times Buddy, Elvis, and Prince stopped to sniff the ground: 991,235,959,326

Times their leashes tangled around telephone poles, trees, and people: 57

Times Buddy, Elvis, and Prince went in different directions all at once: 839 (they are like the Hayes family)

Individual Dog Behavior:

Fights Buddy picked with dogs twice his size: 7

Squirrels that Prince chased up trees: 16

Pools of water that Elvis jumped into: 1

People whom a wet, muddy Elvis jumped onto: 1

(Hint: She has red, curly hair and loves to write. She was also wearing new cargo pants.)

Admiration for best friend has increased dramatically. She walks dogs twice a day AND watches Geoffrey! (Today he spat milk out of his nose.) Jessica must miss me even more than I miss her!

Which is worse?
1. Having Cream of Wheat cereal thrown in your hair or being dragged across a field by an excited dog?
2. Being tied up by a four-year-old or separating two fighting dogs?
3. Having milk sprayed on your shirt or mud pawed on your pants?

Jessica does all of these things! She will get a page in the <u>Hayes Book of World Records</u> for "Toughest Ten-year-old Tackler of Tasks."
(If you can say this very fast twenty times, <u>you</u> will get a page in the <u>Hayes Book of World Records</u>, too.)

P.S. I have decided not to get a dog. Too muddy, too jumpy, too drooly. Jessica says I am not a dog person. Am I a hamster person, like Bethany? A cat person, like Heather? Or a guinea-pig person? A duck person, a rabbit person, or even a worm person?? How will I ever know?

What if I'm a person person? What will I do for a pet then?

I'd have to adopt someone. _Noooooooo!!!!!_ That would mean one more vacation idea to fight over!

P.P.S. I don't want a dog. But I still want a pet. More than ever.

Chapter 4

It depends what kind!

Best Kinds of Water
1. Pools
2. Sprinklers
3. Waterfalls
4. Water dishes for cats, dogs, hamsters, and other pets

Worst Kinds of Water
1. Cold, pouring rain (that prevents you from going to the pool)

2. Cold, pouring rain (that forces you inside musty barn during camp)

3. Cold, pouring rain (that imprisons you in house with grumpy family)

P.S. Spent camp day (8:30 a.m. to 2:30 p.m., or six whole hours, or three hundred and sixty minutes, or twenty-one thousand, six hundred seconds) making Popsicle-stick boxes, macaroni self-portraits, and cornstarch clay. Ugh!! What's next? Meatloaf jewelry?

P.P.S. Bethany agreed with me.

P.P.P.S. Hooray! I have a friend in camp. Well, sort of a friend. A school and pool friend.

P.P.P.P.S. We're in the same group – the Rain Dancers. Why did they have to give us that name? Now everyone blames us for the bad weather!

P.P.P.P.P.S. I like adding extra P's onto the P.S.'s – how long can I continue?

P.P.P.P.P.P.S. Longer than I should.

P.P.P.P.P.P.P.S. Long enough to drive myself crazy.

P.P.P.P.P.P.P.S. If the gloomy rain doesn't drive me crazy first.

P.P.P.P.P.P.P.P.S. This is pathetic.

P.P.P.P.P.P.P.P.P.S. AAAAAAARRRRGGGHH!

It's not fair! There ought to be a law against cold, pouring rain in the summer!

(Ask mother if such a law exists. We can sue the sky! Bring the clouds to court!)

If I had a pet, I could play with it now. A cat and I would cuddle up on the bed. I could talk to a parrot—or watch my hamster go around and around on his wheel. The cold, pouring rain wouldn't bother me if I had a pet.

For a few moments after she closed her journal, Abby stared out her bedroom window at the dark sky. Then she looked at the walls of her room, which were covered with calendars. For the summer months they showed brilliant blue skies, flowers, sailboats, beaches, and mountain sunsets. Not a single downpour or drenched, crabby person among them.

Why didn't they make a Storms of the Northeast Calendar? Or an Ultimate Boredom Calendar? Or a Cold, Wet Tuesday Calendar? If she got to visit a calendar factory this summer, she would ask about it.

The sunshine hanging on her walls did *not* make it easier to bear the rain outside her windows. Abby stood up, stretched, and went downstairs.

No one was around.

She wandered into the kitchen and began opening cupboards. The same old graham crackers and granola bars stared at her. She was sick of them all. "There's nothing to eat, either."

She slumped into a chair and idly picked up the jar of marmalade that Heather had brought back from England.

Maybe Heather was home! Maybe Abby could go play with Marshmallow and her kittens!

She reached for the phone and dialed Heather's number. No one answered. No one answered at Jessica's or Natalie's houses, either. (Not that she really expected them to.)

Where was everyone? Jogging in the rain?

Today was *almost* enough to make her wish for school!!

Well, not quite. Unless it was Ms. Bunder's creative writing class.

This was why she needed a pet. If she had a pet, she wouldn't be bored or lonely.

Suddenly, she had an idea. She picked up the phone again.

"Hello, may I speak to Bethany?"

Bethany was waiting for Abby at the front door. "I'm glad you called," she said. "It's so boring here."

"At my house, too," Abby agreed.

She took off her rain slicker and hung it on a hook in the hallway. She wiped her feet on the mat and shook a few drops of rain from her red hair. The dampness always made it curl more than usual.

Bethany led her through the living room. Three little girls, all blond like Bethany, were sitting in front of the television set.

In the corner of the room, Bethany's mom was talking on the phone and running her hands through her short hair.

She waved hello to Abby, then returned to her phone conversation.

"Let's go up to my room," Bethany whispered. She pointed to the stairs.

The two girls climbed to the second floor. Bethany opened a door at the end of the hallway.

"Here it is," she said.

The bed was neatly made and there was a desk with books arranged on a shelf. The walls were decorated with posters of hamsters, gymnasts, and a framed picture of Brianna.

"There's Blondie." Bethany pointed to a cage on a small table.

A plump golden hamster slept in a nest of wood shavings in the corner of a large cage.

"She's sleeping," Abby said.

"She wakes up when it gets dark," Bethany explained. "Then she'll exercise on her wheel. She runs a couple of miles a day."

"Like my mother!" Abby hadn't known that her mother and hamsters had something in common.

"I can pick her up," Bethany said. "At first she wouldn't let me, but I stroked her fur and offered her pieces of lettuce and parsley. Now she lets me carry her around the house. You have to hold her very gently," she added. "Never squeeze a hamster."

They watched the sleeping hamster for a few moments.

"Isn't she great?" Bethany said.

"What else does she do?" Abby asked.

"She sniffs my hand," Bethany said. "Her whiskers twitch. She makes cute squeaking noises. And once she escaped from her cage and disappeared into the heating ducts. It took us two days to get her back."

"Wow," Abby said. How would her family react if a hamster escaped into the heating ducts? They'd probably argue for two days about the best way to rescue it.

Bethany sank down on the bed, and Abby sat in a chair by the window.

"Does Brianna like hamsters?" She couldn't imagine Brianna in Bethany's room.

"She doesn't like the smell of them." Bethany twisted a lock of her blond hair around her finger. "Besides, we go over to her house most of the time. She has a canopy bed, her own television, and a closet that's bigger than my room."

"She needs it for all her clothes!"

Bethany nodded.

"Is she coming to the diving contest?"

"I hope so," Bethany said. "We're having it on the weekend, aren't we? She won't be in camp then."

Abby tried to imagine how she would feel if both Jessica and Natalie were away all week. She would hate it! It was bad enough not having them in camp with her. Still, she saw them at the pool — when it wasn't raining, of course.

She hoped Bethany didn't feel too unhappy about not seeing Brianna very much.

"You're going to win the contest," Abby said, trying to cheer Bethany up. "I've never seen Mason do anything but belly flop."

"Do you really think so?" Bethany frowned. "Then why is Tyler betting on him?"

She and Tyler were good friends. Bethany had even invited him to her house after school once.

"Probably just because Zach is doing it. You know how boys are. They have to stick together."

"Yuk," Bethany said.

"All for one, and one for all!" Abby recited. "Even if Mason can only do a cannonball!"

Both girls began to laugh.

"You can write a poem about the diving contest," Bethany said, "and give it to the winner as a prize."

"Good idea!" Abby agreed.

"Let's play cards," Bethany suggested. She pulled out a pack with pictures of hamsters on them.

Abby glanced out the window at the dreary, dark

skies. The day was turning out better than she had hoped.

"Do you like every animal?" she asked Bethany.

Bethany thought for a moment. "Hamsters are the best, of course, but I also love dogs, cats, frogs, horses, cows, rabbits, birds, pigs, monkeys, snakes, rhinos, elephants, mice, turtles, fish, and squirrels. But I *hate* spiders! They give me the creeps!"

"I love their webs," Abby said.

Bethany shuddered. "Let's change the subject." She turned over a card. "King of diamonds. Can you beat that?"

"Ace," Abby said.

"That really hurts," Bethany said. "Ouch!"

"Want a Band-Aid?" Abby turned over a five of hearts.

Bethany scooped it up with a six. "No, this is better."

The rain kept falling. Blondie slumbered in her cage.

Abby laid down a jack of spades. Bethany took it with a queen. "This is fun," she said.

"Now that you're winning!" Abby teased. She had lost so many chess games to Alex that it really surprised her if she won any game at all.

Bethany looked pleased. With a best friend like Brianna, she probably didn't get to win very much, either.

"If it stops raining, I'll show you my rabbit," she promised. "We have a hutch in the backyard. I'll even let you feed her."

"That'd be great!"

"We have a fish tank, too. But goldfish are pretty boring," Bethany said. She sat cross-legged on the bed.

"I want a pet I can play with," Abby said. She turned over a ten of diamonds. Bethany took it with a jack.

On the wall was a poster of Bethany in a leotard. She was tumbling on a mat. There was a small silver medal attached to the upper right-hand corner.

As Bethany captured yet another card, Abby gestured toward the poster. "What's that?"

"I won second prize in the state gymnastics competition last year. My parents made the poster for my birthday."

"That's amazing!" Abby cried. "I never knew you were such a good gymnast. You'll have to meet my sister Eva. She's a great athlete, too."

Bethany smiled. "I'd like that."

Chapter 5

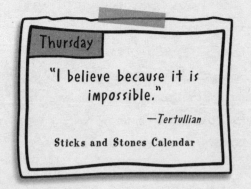

Thursday

"I believe because it is impossible."

—*Tertullian*

Sticks and Stones Calendar

Impossible Beliefs:

1. Abby will find a pet that she loves, and that Alex is not allergic to, and that she can keep in the house.

2. The Hayes family will discover a vacation plan that satisfies everyone.

3. Mason will win the diving contest.

Possible Beliefs:

1. Abby will find a pet that she loves. (Will she be able to keep it?)

2. The Hayes family will go on vacation. (Will more than one person enjoy it?)

3. Bethany will win the diving contest and all the boys will be very, very sorry. (Ha-ha-ha-ha-<u>ha</u>!)

<u>How to Get Pet, Part 2</u>:
a. Handle Bethany's hamster. Feed Bethany's rabbit. (This is what my mother calls "hands-on experience.")
b. Read ads in newspaper.
c. Visit pet store.

Hamster Report:
On Wednesday after camp, Bethany showed me how Blondie sits on her lap, facing toward her. Her fur is very soft! Bethany put her in a special wheel and she rolled all over the floor. We sat and watched Blondie roll for a <u>long</u> time. She nibbled, squeaked, twitched, sniffed, and chewed. Then she went to sleep again.
Note to self: Do <u>not</u> give Blondie a page in the <u>Hayes Book of World Records</u> for "Most Exciting Pet."

Rabbit Report:

Bethany also has a rabbit in her backyard. The rabbit's name is Binkie. (If
Bethany had a third pet, what would she
name it? Beanie? Bunny? Barry? Boo-
Boo?) I fed Binkie lettuce, carrot greens,
and cabbage. Binkie kicked me very hard.
And tried to bite my hand.

Note to self: Forget about hands-on experience! In future, choose hands-<u>off</u> experience,
instead!

Newspaper and Pet Store Report:

The dogs, cats, and horses advertised in
the paper cost hundreds of dollars!

The pets in the store need expensive
shots, cages, and toys.

Conclusion:

It is harder to find a pet than I
thought! But I can do it! Nothing will stop
me. Will put self in <u>Hayes Book of</u>
<u>World Records</u> for "Most Persistent Pet
Pursuit."

Weather Report:
Rain, rain, go away,
Come again another day.
Abby, Jessica, and Natalie want to play.
Bethany wants to practice her dives —
This cold, wet weather is ruining our lives!

On Friday, the rain stopped. After camp, Abby met her friends at the pool. She had exciting news.

"My parents are pitching a tent in our backyard tonight. We're going to have an end-of-the-rain barbecue and my mom said I can invite three friends for a sleepover!"

"It's really fun," Jessica said to Natalie. "We did it last year. Alex wanted to join us. He got scared by an owl and ran inside before it was even dark."

Abby laughed. "Just say 'Whooooo? Whooooo?' when you see him." She laid down her towel on a beach chair. "What do you think? Will your parents let you come?"

"My mom will say yes," Jessica said. "Especially since it's a weekend night. What about you, Natalie?"

Natalie scratched a mosquito bite on her leg. "I don't know. . . ." Her parents were strict about things like sleepovers and parties. "I don't even have a sleeping bag."

"Don't worry, the Hayes family has lots of sleeping bags," Abby said.

"They might let me," Natalie said slowly. "If I promise to get at least six hours of sleep."

Jessica and Abby exchanged glances.

"Last year we stayed up pretty late," Abby warned. "We had comic books and flashlights and lots of snacks. My dad calls it Camp Hayes. He and my mom checked on us a lot."

"I'll tell my parents that," Natalie said. She fished in her pocket and pulled out a quarter. "I'll call them on the pay phone and ask if I can come."

"Who's the third person?" Jessica asked as Natalie walked away. "Alex again?"

Abby pointed to the diving board, where Bethany stood poised at the edge. As she and Jessica watched, Bethany raised her arms gracefully above her head and dived into the water.

"Did you know that Bethany won a silver medal in a statewide gymnastics contest?" Abby said. "I bet even Brianna never did that!"

"You're inviting Bethany?" Jessica said.

"Yes, why not?"

"She's nice, but—"

"But???"

Jessica didn't say anything.

"Is it because of Brianna?" Abby asked.

"Maybe."

"It's not fair to judge someone by her friends!" Abby cried. She was surprised. Jessica was usually kind to others.

"You're right," Jessica mumbled. "Forget I said anything."

The two girls looked toward the diving board again. It was Mason's turn. He lumbered out to the end, then cannonballed into the water.

At the edge of the pool, Tyler and Zach applauded wildly.

"It's weird," Abby said. "Have you ever seen Mason do anything but belly flops and cannonballs?"

"No," Jessica agreed. "But what's weird about that?"

"Zach and Tyler seem so sure he's going to win."

"He practices his dives in secret?" Jessica suggested.

Abby shook her head. "*Where?* He's always here. Look, now he's slurping up a snow cone."

"Hey!" It was Natalie. She was running toward

Jessica and Abby with a bag of popcorn clutched in one hand. Kernels spilled out behind her as she ran. "My parents said yes!"

"YES!" Abby and Jessica jumped up and hugged her. More popcorn spilled on the ground.

"I had to promise to sleep," Natalie said. She took a handful of popcorn and offered the bag to her friends. "Or else I'm going to have to act very wide awake tomorrow."

"You can do it!" Jessica cried. "Aren't you the best actor in fifth grade?"

"Except for Brianna," Bethany said. A towel was tied around her waist. She twirled her goggles as she spoke.

"Brianna *is* a really good actor," Abby admitted. "She and Natalie stole the show when we did *Peter Pan*."

Natalie nodded in agreement, but Jessica was silent.

Abby took a breath. "I'm having a sleepover to-night in a tent in my backyard. Jessica and Natalie are coming. Do you want to join us?"

Bethany's face lit up. "I'd love to."

"Will your parents let you?" Natalie asked. She held out the popcorn to Bethany.

"Oh, sure. I sleep over at Brianna's all the time. She has the *best* room."

Bethany slipped her feet into sandals and picked up her beach bag. "I promised my mom to help out with my annoying sisters for an hour today. I'll see you later."

Abby picked up the sunscreen and began applying it to her shoulders. "Speaking of annoying sisters . . . "

"Are your SuperSibs going to be around tonight?" Natalie asked.

"Of course!" Abby sighed dramatically. "Unless they have parties or sleepovers with *their* friends."

Jessica stared at the ground.

"What's wrong?" Abby asked.

"I hope Bethany doesn't brag about Brianna the entire night!" Jessica blurted. "I don't think I can stand it!"

"She won't," Abby promised. "At least she didn't when I was at her house."

"'Brianna has the *best* room,'" Jessica mimicked.

"She has everything but a swimming pool," Abby said. "It *does* sound great."

"I can't believe you said that, Abby Hayes!"

"Well, you said Bethany was really nice!" Abby reminded her best friend. "Remember?"

"I didn't think you'd invite her to our Camp Hayes sleepover!"

"Well, I did!"

"An argument! An argument!" Zach interrupted gleefully. He and Tyler crowded around the girls.

"We're not arguing; we're discussing our sleepover," Jessica mumbled. She didn't look at Abby as she spoke.

"A sleepover? Where?" Tyler grabbed a huge handful of popcorn from Natalie's bag and emptied it into his mouth all at once.

"We're pitching a tent in my backyard," Abby said. "We're going to stay up all night."

The two boys glanced at each other. "Enjoy yourselves while you can."

"What do you mean by that?" Natalie demanded.

"Just wait until Mason wins the contest."

"Do you have eyes?" Abby retorted. "Have you seen Bethany dive?"

Zach shrugged. "She's okay."

"She's *way* better than Mason!"

"So?"

"How can he win?" Jessica asked.

Zach and Tyler grinned. "Boy power."

"Boy power will make him a better diver?" Abby said.

"Sure." Tyler tried to grab another handful of popcorn from Natalie's bag, but she yanked it out of his reach.

Laughing loudly, the two boys walked away.

Abby frowned. "They can't make Mason a better diver in one week. What are they planning?"

"A body double?" Natalie said.

"Secret coaching?" Jessica suggested.

Abby shook her head. "They have a secret. We have to find it out."

Chapter 6

Friday   Still (almost Saturday)

"Oh Sleep! it is a gentle thing,
Beloved from pole to pole . . ."

— Samuel Taylor Coleridge

Down Pillow Calendar

Sleep is not beloved from pole to pole of this tent! All four of us girls want to stay up as late as we can! Whoever stays up all night will win a prize! (We haven't decided what it is yet.)

9:45 p.m. Live! From Camp Hayes!
We now bring you a report from the Hayes family tent, which has been pitched between the flower garden and the tomato patch. Four girls in pajamas are sitting in a circle, playing cards. It is not yet clear whether Bethany or Jessica will win. (It is

very clear that Natalie and Abby will lose!)

For dinner, we had hot dogs, hamburgers, potato salad, and watermelon. Bethany brought her own hot dogs made of tofu. She became a vegetarian because she loves animals so much. (If there were spiderburgers, though, she would probably eat them.)

Bethany told us that you can make tofu meatloaf, tofu fish cakes, tofu bread and cookies, and even tofu ice cream.

Ugh!

(Question: How can something that looks like a square of squishy white jelly taste like meat, fish, grains, or ice cream? A mystery of science. Also a mystery why anyone eats it.)

During dinner, Natalie updated the Hayes family on her chemistry experiments. Bethany talked about Blondie and Binkie. Jessica described how Geoffrey floated boats in the toilet today.

Inviting Bethany to the sleepover was a brilliant masterstroke on part of Abby Hayes. Bethany talked nonstop about pets, how lovable they are, and how much fun it is to take care of them. She said that she feeds, cleans, and plays with her pets without any help from her mom or dad. The Hayes parents were very impressed.

Yay, Bethany! Yay, Bethany! Yay, Bethany!

After dinner, Eva organized a game of volleyball. Paul Hayes turned on the hose and the girls ran under the sprinkler to cool off. Then they sat on the porch and sang songs. Alex challenged all four girls to a game of chess. (They lost.) Isabel made popcorn for everyone. Camp Hayes is the best!

Vacation Idea: If no one can agree on where they want to go, we stay home and camp out in the backyard for a week!

Alex thinks this is a great idea. If two of us agree, does it break the tie???

10:18 p.m. Emptying out our bags in the tent. What did everyone bring (besides toothbrushes, clean underwear, and other boring things)?

Bethany: candy, face glitter, hair ornaments, nail polish, mirror, pack of cards, and photos of Blondie.

Natalie: candy, books, powerful flashlight, and tape recorder to record nature sounds.

Jessica: candy, asthma inhaler, telescope, drawing pad, and favorite stuffed animal.

Abby: candy, earrings, three calendars, and purple journal — _of course_!

10:19 p.m. Eating candy.

10:27 p.m. Bethany does our nails.

10:44 p.m. Eating candy.

11:02 p.m. Jessica sketches funny pictures of us, our classmates, and families.

11:11 p.m. Eating candy.

11:39 p.m. Natalie imitates the boys in our class. She pretends she is Tyler on his computer and Zach collecting cheat codes. She burps the alphabet just like Mason! (Maybe after the diving contest we will have burping contest?)

11:44 p.m. Eating can — you know what we're eating!

11:46 p.m. Pet discussion. I pull out classified ads. Natalie, Jessica, Bethany, and I look through them. Just in case.

11:47 p.m. No pets under $300 in newspaper today.

11:48 p.m. Natalie notices ad for free bunnies to good home. I remember hands-on experience with Binkie and shake my head.

11:49 p.m. How am I going to find a pet? Will I ever get the chance to show my family that I can take care of a pet on my own? My prospects look bleak. Am about to sink into despair.

11:50 p.m. Bethany suddenly cries out, "You can visit Lily with me!"

Lily is a friend of Bethany's who has eighteen pets! She rescues animals and might have one that needs a home. If I promise to take good care of it, Lily will give it to me for free.

11:54 p.m. Hooray, Bethany! Hooray,

Bethany! <u>Hooray</u>, Bethany! I can't wait to visit Lily. Bethany says she's going to see her on Sunday.

12:00 Midnight!! Outside in pajamas and bare feet. Looking at the stars through Jessica's telescope. Natalie sets up tape recorder.

Natalie says night sky looks like one big electronic game. If so, Zach and Tyler probably have cheat codes.

12:15 a.m. Running around yard. Swinging on swing set. Playing tag in the dark.

12:56 a.m. Back in tent. Lights out in Hayes family home. Everyone, even Isabel, who sometimes stays up all night, in bed. Mom comes to check on us one last time. She says, "Get some sleep, girls, <u>please</u>!"

Number of candy wrappers hidden as we heard her approach: hundreds!

Giggles when Mom told us to go to sleep: dozens!

Promises to sleep made with crossed fingers: 4

1:30 a.m. Natalie asleep. Book lying over face. Must have fallen asleep in the middle of a sentence.

Three people now awake: me, Jessica, and Bethany.

2:01 a.m. Eating candy.

3:18 a.m. Bethany tells terrifying story about severed head. As she finishes, we hear gruesome howling outside tent. Bethany whispers that it sounds like wolves.

Panic and terror. Can wolves break into Hayes family tent? Can they eat through mosquito netting? Do they want to eat us?

We stare at one another with tears in our eyes.

"I'm sorry I thought you were a bragging Brianna clone," Jessica says to Bethany.

"You're all nicer than Brianna said," Bethany tells us.

"I'm sorry I ate so much candy," I say, clutching my stomach.

The wolves are coming closer. We arm ourselves with weapons at hand. Bethany

takes hairbrush and mirror, Jessica gathers
remaining candy (to distract wolves), and
I pick up book that has slid off Natalie.

"Charge!" Jessica hisses, and we rush
bravely out of the tent.

3:41 a.m. Still alive! We are safe in tent.
No wolves at all. Instead, three boylike
shapes (suspiciously similar to Mason, Tyler,
and Zach) rushed from yew bushes when I
tossed book at them.

Question: Who were they?
Question: What were they doing there?
Question: What were they doing there at
3:00 a.m.?

5:56 a.m. We have discussed the above
questions for over two hours and we still
have no answers!
6:02 a.m. Natalie still sleeping. Jessica's
eyes close, then snap awake.
6:18 a.m. Getting tired but we can't go to
sleep now!

6:19 a.m. We strip off nail polish and paint nails again.

6:34 a.m. And again.

6:55 a.m. And again.

7:22 a.m. And a — oh, forget it!

7:29 a.m. Natalie wakes up. We go into house and make blueberry waffles. We decide that this is the prize for staying up all night, as well as Natalie's prize for sleeping through everything.

Dad sits at table drinking coffee. He and Mom slept "solidly" from 1:00 a.m. to 7:00 a.m. (Question: Why not sleep liquidly? Or squishily? Or dryly?)

He didn't hear the howling wolves. He didn't know about our courageous defense of Camp Hayes. But he isn't surprised that we stayed up all night!

Pounds of candy we have eaten: 6
Ghost stories we have told: 18
Card games we have played: 39
Hours we (except Natalie) have slept: 0

9:35 a.m. The sleepover is over. Mom says it should be called a "_No_ Sleep-over." Natalie was the only one who slept at all. (Good thing! Now her parents won't be mad. They might let her do it again.)

9:36 a.m. I am not tired at all! I'm just going to write a little more in my journal before I Rollerblade with Ale...

Chapter 7

Sunday

"You can never plan the future by the past."

— *Edmund Burke*

Starfish Calendar

Why would you want to? If you planned the future by the past, you'd do the same thing over and over again!!!

Today will be different from yesterday. Today I will be awake.

Yesterday, after my friends left, I slept the entire day and night! Will put self in <u>Hayes Book of World Records</u> for "Sleepiest Snooze After Sleepless Sleepover."

Today I am going to visit Bethany's friend Lily and her eighteen pets. Maybe she has an extra one for me!

The truck pulled into the driveway.

"We're here, girls," said Bethany's dad.

They had driven for an hour until the roads became narrow and quiet and the houses were far apart. Now all around were grassy meadows bordered by trees. At the top of a hill sat a red house with vegetable gardens surrounding it.

Bethany's dad reached over to open the door. "Careful getting out," he warned Abby. "It's a bit of a drop."

Abby unbuckled her seat belt and jumped to the ground. "Thanks for the ride!"

"Bye, Dad!" Bethany hopped down and slammed the door shut.

Her father winced.

"Oops, sorry, I forgot. He hates it when the door slams," she explained to Abby.

Bethany waved as her father backed slowly onto the road. The truck bed was filled with lumber that her father was delivering to a cousin's house.

The two girls began to walk toward the house on the hill.

A door flew open. Five dogs of all sizes and shapes ran onto the front deck.

Bethany waved. "Hi, Boomer! Hi, Patches! Hi, April! Hi, Sparky! Hi, Gloria!" she cried.

The dogs barked wildly in greeting and wagged their tails. From inside the house came loud screeches.

"Lily has three birds, five dogs, two cows, one goat, and seven cats." Bethany's eyes sparkled. "But the macaw is making all the noise."

A small goat wandered over. "That's Margaret. She's very friendly. She won't butt or bite like other goats do."

Abby reached out and touched the goat's head. Its hair was light brown and coarse.

"All Lily's pets are friendly," Bethany said. "Some of them are practically human."

Abby couldn't wait to meet Lily. She had never seen so many animals living in one place outside of a zoo. None of them looked mean or scared or dirty, either. Lily took in abandoned animals and gave them a home. Bethany had told her all about it on the drive over.

Abby wondered how Lily found the time for homework and soccer games, Rollerblading and school plays. She was probably so busy taking care of her animals that she never went to sleepovers.

An older woman with gray hair in a ponytail came from inside the house. She wore a blue bathing suit and shiny red shorts. Her bare feet were in flip-flops.

"You're here!" she said, with a smile. "Mona is waiting to see you." She turned and marched toward the back.

"Come on!" Bethany grabbed Abby's arm.

"Who's Mona?" Abby said. "And where's Lily?"

Bethany pointed straight ahead at the woman. "That's her!"

"Mona??"

"Mona's the cow! That's *Lily*!"

Abby stumbled and almost fell. Lily wasn't ten years old. She had gray hair. She was older than Abby's mother. Bethany had a grown-up friend!

Abby didn't know too many fifth-graders with grown-up friends. She was friends with Heather, but Heather wasn't that much older than Isabel or Eva.

"Look!" Bethany said. There was admiration and pride in her voice.

Ahead of them, Lily had stopped in the middle of a field. She was standing next to a sleek and healthy cow, which nuzzled her hand.

"I've had her since she was a baby," Lily explained

when the girls caught up with her. "Fed her from a bottle. She's a Jersey Holstein mix. Not a milk cow. The farmer would have sent her away to be fattened for someone's dinner."

"Mona is why I don't eat meat anymore," Bethany said to Abby. "Isn't she beautiful?"

Mona lifted her head and turned to Bethany with dark, shining eyes. As if she understood what had been said, she rubbed her head back and forth against Bethany's hip.

"She's saying hello!" Bethany cried in delight. She didn't seem to care that her pants now had a dirt stain where Mona rubbed her head.

"She's happy to see you," Lily said to Bethany. "She missed you."

"Pet her," Bethany encouraged Abby. "She loves it when you stroke her neck."

Abby petted Mona's neck. It was smooth and soft. Would Mona rub her head against *her* leg?

She didn't.

"If you come again, she'll recognize you," Bethany said. "This is only the second time she's said hello to me like that."

"Does Mona say hello to Brianna?" Abby asked.

She tried to imagine Brianna letting a cow — even a clean, beautiful, and friendly one like Mona — rub its head against her pants leg and failed.

Bethany looked away. "Brianna's never visited here."

"Oh." Abby felt bad for Bethany. Jessica and she had different interests, but they shared them. Bethany knew all about Brianna, but Brianna didn't seem to know much about Bethany.

A black-and-white calf ambled over to the girls.

"Here's my baby," Lily cooed. "Hello, Martha."

"What happened to her nose?" Bethany asked. The calf's nose was mottled pink. It looked tender and sore.

"She got a touch of sunburn," Lily said. "Didn't know enough to stay out of the sun." She held out her fingers to the calf, who began sucking on them like a pacifier. "I have to keep suntan lotion on her now and make sure she stays in the shade."

"Wow," Abby said. "I never knew cows got sunburned."

"They do," Lily said. Gently, she withdrew her fingers from the calf's mouth. There were white, milky stains on her hand and wrist. "She's just a baby and still learning."

"Lily has the greatest dogs!" Abby said to her family later that day. The Hayes family was on the back porch enjoying ice cream with raspberries. "One of them was all white with a black patch over her left eye! She made the funniest faces at me!"

After an hour at Lily's house, Abby loved dogs again. She loved all animals. Lily's animals were so happy and playful — even the cows! Mona and Martha were so gentle and loving; their eyes were so expressive. Abby wished . . . she wished . . . she wished . . .

"Could we keep a cow in the backyard?" Abby asked.

"A *cow*?" her mother repeated in disbelief.

"In the backyard?" her father said.

"Are you crazy?" Eva cried. "Do you know how much food they eat?"

"And how much manure they create?" Isabel demanded.

"I don't want a cow in the backyard!" Alex cried.

"Okay, okay," Abby said. She knew when she was

outnumbered. She spooned another bite of ice cream and raspberries into her mouth. "I was just joking, anyway," she mumbled.

Visiting Lily's house hadn't solved her problem. Abby hadn't come home with a pet. Judging from her family's reaction, that was a good thing. What if she *had* brought a cow back? Or a goat? Or a macaw? Or even that white dog with the black patch?

Olivia Hayes clapped her hands to get everyone's attention. "We need to talk about the family vacation," she said. "Are there any new ideas?"

Isabel stood up. "Alex and I had a chat yesterday," she announced. "We decided to combine our vacation plans. I'd love to visit a science and technology museum, and Alex says that he wants to see Revolutionary War battlefields."

"Yep," Alex agreed.

"So our idea wins," Isabel concluded. "We have a clear majority."

"Not so fast!" Eva put down her spoon to frown at her twin. "Mom and I have also been talking! We came up with a new plan that *both* of us love: hiking in the mountains."

Abby stared at her family in dismay. She had been so busy that she hadn't even thought about the family vacation! Meanwhile, her mother and Eva and Isabel and Alex had paired up, leaving her out in the cold. Now her vacation hopes were doomed.

"Don't worry," her father whispered, giving her arm a quick squeeze. He cleared his throat and addressed the family. "I've been doing research on the Internet. There's a wonderful beach not too far from Grandma Emma's house. I could relax, Abby could visit, and the rest of you could find museums, antique stores, and hiking trails. There might even be a calendar store in the area."

He beamed triumphantly, as if daring them to find fault with his plan. "And Grandma Emma is my favorite relative by marriage," he added.

"*Yes!*" Abby cried, throwing her arms around her father.

"No!" cried Isabel and Alex and Eva.

Olivia Hayes shook her head. "I disagree, Paul. Much as I wish I were wrong, there are several things you've overlooked. . . ."

Arguments erupted from every side of the table.

Abby's head ached. Had anyone ever run away from home because of too many arguments over a family vacation?

Abby picked up her journal and opened it on her lap under the table.

Before, six people had six ideas. Now six people have three ideas. Will this make the Hayes family vacation decision any easier?
Guess the answer correctly and win a free trip to a desert island!

Should all the Hayeses vacation on separate desert islands? I would rather be stranded on a dessert island! A dessert island with lots of pets!!!

Chapter 8

I did what I was afraid of doing. No, it didn't involve spiders, diving contests, or confronting "wolves." This was something much bigger. I was so afraid of it that I never even dreamed I'd actually do it!

I adopted a pet.

Without my family's permission or knowledge.

Six Easy Steps to Getting Your Own Pet

1. Walk past Heather's apartment.

2. Wave hello when you see her on the porch.

3. Say yes when she invites you inside to play with Marshmallow's kittens, los gatitos.

4. Fall in love with a gray kitten with pale blue eyes who purrs whenever he's near you.

5. Listen sympathetically when Heather tells you how hard it is to find homes for Marshmallow's kittens.

6. Generously offer to take one home.

P.S. When Heather says, "This is okay with your parents, isn't it?", nod and smile as if it is. Don't actually lie — but don't exactly tell the truth, either. Stay in what my father calls "the gray area." A good name for a kitten? "Gray Area." No. It's not cute and cuddly enough. (Sounds like a living room floor.)

I think I will call him Secret. Or Smoky. Or George. Or...

Who cares what I call him? I have my own kitten! Yay! Hooray! He was waiting for me right next door.

<u>Things I Love About My Kitten</u>:
1. When he purrs.
2. When he sits in my lap.
3. When he plays with me.
4. His silky gray fur.
5. His pale blue eyes.
6. His little pink tongue.
7. His long, waving tail.

I will tell my parents VERY SOON. They will see how lovable he is! They will see that I take great care of him! They will give me permission to keep him. In the meantime, I have things under control. I'm taking care of my kitten all by myself.

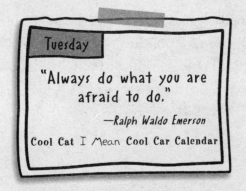

Tuesday

"Always do what you are afraid to do."

—Ralph Waldo Emerson

Cool Cat I Mean Cool Car Calendar

(Haven't had time to look up new quote; am too busy with kitten.)

Things I Have Done That I Was Afraid to Do:
1. Adopted kitten.
2. Hid kitten in room.
3. Purchased litter box, cat food, toys, and dishes and brought them up to my room without family noticing.
4. Stored open can of cat food in refrigerator.
5. Pretended cat food was a surprise for Bethany.

Things I Haven't Done That I'm Not Afraid of Doing:
1. Named the kitten. What shall I call him? Yum-Yum, Cuddles, Silly Putty, Slobber, Sweetums, Thelma, Billy Bob, Gorgeous, Samantha, Cyril, Albertine, Purple Lion? I will call him Kitten for now.

<u>Things I Haven't Done That I'm Afraid</u>
<u>of Doing</u>:
1. Told my parents about Kitten.

Last night Alex was sneezing a lot. Was it pollen? Or cat hair in the air?
I feel very guilty. So guilty that I almost said that I'd visit a science and technology museum on our vacation!
But I still didn't tell Mom and Dad.
P.S. Natalie called. Wonder what she wants. Am too busy to call back.

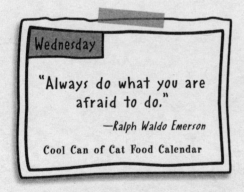

Wednesday

"Always do what you are afraid to do."

—Ralph Waldo Emerson

Cool Can of Cat Food Calendar

(Just kidding, ha-ha. It's really the Cool Car Calendar.)

Why?

Once you do what you are afraid to do, you get stuck doing something that you are even _more_ afraid to do! Like telling your parents the truth!

How much longer can I keep this secret up?

If no one has noticed Kitten yet, it's only because the members of the Hayes family are so busy that they're never home.

Still ... No disasters yet! I'm taking great care of Kitten. Lily will be proud of me. So will Bethany. And my family, of course.

Kitten wakes me up in the morning by jumping on my head and getting tangled in my hair (which is already tangled enough)!

This morning he dug his claws into my face, too.

"YEEEEOOOOUUUUCCCHH!"

Dad (knocking at door): Is everything okay, Abby?

Me (hiding Kitten under covers): Yes!

Kitten: Meow!

Dad: What's that I hear?

Me: What's what you what?

Kitten: Meow!

Dad: That!

Me: Oh, that! Just a new band I'm listening to. Heather lent me the CD.

Kitten: Meow!

Dad: Interesting sound. (Goes downstairs to start breakfast.)

A close call!

Must not let my parents accidentally find out about Kitten. This is the kind of news that makes parents turn purple and start sputtering with a) annoyance, b) anger, or c) more anger. Must carefully prepare them. Must cleverly lead them to think that a kitten is what _they_ want most!

Kitten cuddles: 324

Kitten scratches: 12

Kitten accidents (don't ask what kind): 5

Lies I have told about Kitten: 126

Amount of money I have spent so far on Kitten: $48.37

(Uh-oh! I'm running out of money. Will I have to baby-sit Geoffrey to feed my Kitten?)

Times I have cleaned litter box so my room wouldn't stink: 7

Cans of deodorizing spray I have emptied: 2

Have new name for Kitten. Trouble.

(Natalie called me _again_! Must remember to call her back.)

Thursday | very early morning

"Always do what you are afraid ..."

<u>Oh, all right! Shut up! I'll do it already!!!</u>

Chapter 9

Thursday · Still early morning

"Afraid? Of whom am I afraid?"
— *Emily Dickinson*

Spiked Hair Calendar

What do <u>you</u> think?

Hint: Two parents who have not yet given permission for their ten-year-old daughter to keep a pet. (Even though I can handle everything by myself.)

Another hint: Two adults with the power to ban my kitten from the house forever.

Okay, here I go! I will bravely go forth and face my doom. If I can find Trouble. He must know that something bad is about to happen. He's hiding under the bed where

I can't reach him, and he won't come out.

At 7:30 A.M., Abby entered the kitchen carrying a small gray kitten in her arms. There were clumps of dust in her tangled hair and scratches on her face and arms.

Her family stared at her, openmouthed.

"This is Trouble," Abby said, trying in vain to hold him. The kitten squirmed free from her arms onto the table, upsetting a small jug of milk.

"It certainly is," Paul Hayes agreed, mopping up the table with a napkin.

Her mother jumped away and examined the skirt of her pale blue silk suit. "Abby, I just got this suit back from the cleaners. . . . "

"Sorry, Mom!" Abby tried to scoop up Trouble, but he leaped off the table and ran under the sideboard.

"Kitty! Kitty!" Alex sneezed.

"Whose cat is this?" Eva demanded.

"Mine," Abby began. "My cat, Trouble —"

"Yours?" her mother said.

"Well named," her father added.

"Why does Abby get to have a cat and I don't?" Isabel demanded.

"No one has a cat," her mother replied, sinking back into her chair. "At least I didn't know that anyone did."

Abby lifted her head defiantly. "He's my cat and I love him."

"I thought there was a funny smell coming from your room," her father murmured.

Under the sideboard, Trouble crouched fearfully. He wasn't planning to move anytime soon. He had obviously seen enough of the Hayes family.

Maybe that was better, Abby thought. That way he couldn't knock anything over. Or scratch anyone. As long as Trouble kept quiet, she had a chance to convince her family to let her keep him.

Her mother fanned her face with a napkin. "How long has he been here?"

Abby took a breath. "Four days."

"Four days!" Isabel screamed. "That's practically a year!"

"Who bought the litter box? And the cat food? And the kitty litter?" her father asked.

"I did, Mom and Dad. I spent all my money on my

cat. Not only that, but I fed him, and petted him, and played with him. Didn't I take good care of him?"

Her father nodded in agreement. "It looks like it."

"Can I keep him?" Abby cried. "*Please?*"

Her parents exchanged glances.

"What a way to start the morning," her father said.

"I'll keep everything really clean!" Abby promised. "I'll empty the litter box every day and Trouble will stay in my room so he doesn't tear up the furniture or give Alex an allergic reaction."

"We need time to think more about this," her mother said.

"Please? Please? *Please?* This is Trouble's only home. He has nowhere to go if you cast him out into the cold." Abby hoped her mother hadn't listened to the weather report. The temperature was supposed to reach 85 degrees by afternoon.

Her mother sighed. "I guess for now, it's okay."

"Mom! I love you! You're the best!" Abby almost hugged her mother but remembered just in time that she was covered with dust and her mother was dressed for work. Instead, she blew her a kiss.

Isabel shook her head in disgust. "I've been begging for a cat for years. Now Abby gets one just like that! It's no fair!"

"I'd rather have a dog," Eva said. "We could keep a dog outside. I'd take it running every night. It wouldn't bother Alex's allergies."

"Aaaachooo!" Alex sneezed. "I'm not allergic to anything! I want a dog and a cat *and* mice! Aaaaachooo!"

Olivia Hayes checked her watch. "I'm off to work. Arguing in court will be easy after this. Your father will deal with all problems from now on."

"Lucky me," Paul Hayes said, pouring himself another cup of coffee.

Abby got down on her hands and knees to coax Trouble out from under the sideboard.

"Well, this explains the cat food in the refrigerator," her sister Isabel said, getting up from the table. "I thought it was the latest fifth-grade fad."

Quick News Flash!
Abby Hayes did not get in as much trouble as she thought for keeping Trouble. Will put self in Hayes Book of World Records as "Luckiest Ten-Year-Old in World."

Or did my parents recognize how responsible I've been?

P.S. What is it with older sisters? They are always ready to believe the worst of their younger sisters. Isabel actually thought I ate cat food! UGH!!

Chapter 10

Thursday Later

"Truth is stranger than fiction."

This is what Natalie said on the phone when I finally called her back. She wouldn't say any more. She has called an all-friends meeting this evening.

She loves mystery! But I hate suspense! What is she going to tell us? It'd better be good. I'd rather be with my kitten, but I can't say no to my friends.

Abby swooped around the fountain on her Rollerblades and came to a halt in front of an empty bench. No one had arrived yet. She hoped they weren't going to be late. Checking her watch, she took off her helmet and placed it under the bench. When she glanced up again, Natalie and Jessica were approaching.

"Thank goodness you're here!" Jessica cried, waving to Abby. She had a bag of marshmallows in one hand and a bottle of water in the other.

Natalie wore gym shorts and an old T-shirt. Her short hair was uncombed. She was wearing a blue backpack.

Jessica sat down on the bench next to Abby. "Natalie wouldn't tell me anything on the way over! She insisted on saving it until we were all together."

"It's too much to explain to just one person," Natalie said, slipping off her backpack.

"Is it animal, vegetable, or mineral?" Jessica asked.

"Animal."

"A pet?" Abby said.

Natalie shook her head.

"I can't stand the suspense!" Abby cried.

"Me, neither," Jessica said.

Natalie unzipped her backpack and took out a tape recorder. "Remember how I wanted to record nature sounds during our sleepover?"

"You set up the tape recorder and then went to

sleep. You missed all the excitement," Abby said.

"I didn't miss *all* the excitement." Natalie smiled mysteriously as she pressed the PLAY button on the tape recorder. "Wait till you hear *this*!"

Tape Transcript (As Written Down by Abby, as Best She Can Remember, in Her Journal, an Hour Later)

Background Night Noises: Crickets chirp. Dogs bark. Cars pass. Muffled giggles. A blare of music from the street. More muffled giggles.

This goes on for a while. Quite a while. A very long while. Until, suddenly ... Footsteps approach. Twigs crackle. Thump. Thud. Thump.

Zach (hushed secretive voice): Do you have the jar of spiders?

Mason (reassuring): Right here. I'm keeping it very safe. Did you find more?

Zach: Yes.

Mason: That makes thirteen.

Tyler (gleeful): We'll let them loose on the

diving board right before Bethany's dive. She'll be so terrified that she'll fall into the water and lose the contest.

Zach (very gleeful): Who would have thought that Bethany faints at the sight of an itty-bitty spider?

Mason (extremely gleeful): No one will ever figure out what we did!

Tyler, Mason, and Zach: Ha-ha-ha-ha-ha!!!

Crickets chirp. Dogs bark. Cars pass. Thud. Bump. Crash.

Zach (annoyed): Watch it!

Mason (also annoyed): Watch it, yourself!

Tyler (urgent): Sssshh!! We don't want them to hear us. At least not yet. (Pauses.) Do you think they'll find out? I don't want Bethany to know I told everyone her secret.

Mason (confident): _Never!_

Zach: It's almost time! Are you ready? We'll give them a warm-up scare.

Tyler and Mason: Yes.

Terrifying howls of "wolves." Frightened whimpers of girls. And then ...

Jessica (bold, fearless, daring, confident, heroic): <u>CHARGE!!!!!!</u>

We end the transcript here as the rest of the story is well known to the audience. However, we listened to the end of the tape, anyway.

Some of the sounds we heard:
—Thud of a large, heavy book being thrown into the bushes.
—"Wolves" fleeing through the bushes and out onto the street.
—Three fearless friends returning to the tent to discuss the battle and polish their nails (again).

"You never know *what* you're going to hear when you record the great outdoors," Natalie said as she switched off the tape recorder.

The three girls were silent for a few minutes.

"I *knew* it was them," Abby said after a while.

"The wolves, I mean. But I can't believe what they're planning with the spiders!"

"I never knew that boys could sink that low," Jessica agreed.

"Mason's going to sink like a stone," Abby said, "but he'll still win the diving contest if he lets a spider loose near Bethany!"

"We have to confront them with the evidence!" Natalie held up the tape. "They won't be able to deny this!"

"No, they won't!" Jessica and Abby shouted.

The girls high-fived one another.

Then, suddenly, Abby shook her head. "Playing the tape won't stop the boys. They'll pretend it's a joke."

"You're right," Natalie agreed. "I can see Mason sneering now."

She patted the tape in her pocket. "Even if the boys deny everything, I'm keeping the evidence safe. Just in case we need it."

Jessica took a swig of water from her bottle. "Maybe Bethany won't notice the spiders?"

"She spots them a mile away," Abby said. "She's always on the lookout for them."

"Then we should warn her!" Jessica cried.

"That'll backfire." Abby was getting to know Bethany well. "If we tell her about the spiders, she'll refuse to dive."

Natalie looked glum. "Why can't Bethany be afraid of elephants? Or giraffes? Or walruses? Or anything too big to stick on the end of a diving board!"

"Why did Tyler tell Mason and Zach that Bethany is afraid of spiders?" Jessica added. "I thought he was her friend!"

"He wanted to impress the other boys?" Abby suggested. "Or maybe he bet a computer game on Mason."

"Will the boys *really* do it? Won't they decide that it's too mean?" Jessica said.

The three friends looked at one another.

"They're going to do it!" they chorused.

With a sigh, Jessica opened the bag of marshmallows. "Anyone want one?"

Abby shook her head. "I like them toasted. Plain marshmallows remind me of pillows."

"Sugar pillows," Jessica said. "Yum."

Natalie took three from the bag. "I love these," she said. "My mom never buys them."

"At least we've solved the mystery of the wolves,"

Jessica said after a while. "I wonder how they knew we were having Camp Hayes?"

"Elementary. We told them at the pool. Remember?" Natalie took another three marshmallows from the bag.

"Oh, right. Abby and I were arguing about Bethany. Now we're worrying about how to protect her." Jessica shook her head. "Are you sure she can't be told?"

"Positive!" Abby reached for her helmet. "Our best bet is to stop the boys."

She fastened the helmet strap under her chin and stood up on her Rollerblades.

"We can't let the boys outwit us," Abby said. "Bethany deserves to win. I want her to beat Mason. Now more than ever!"

Her friends nodded in agreement. "We *have* to find a solution."

Chapter 11

Friday afternoon

"Let sleeping dogs lie."

Happy Hamster Calendar

And let sleeping cats alone, too! Trouble is curled up on my pillow. I am not going to wake him up to play. Instead I am going to the pool for the first time this week!

I can't wait! The diving contest is this weekend. Natalie, Jessica, and I have to foil the boys' plot! Quickly!

Abby hurried into the pool area and flung her towel and bag on the grass where her friends usually gathered. They weren't there. Nor were they on the slide, in the water, or at the Snack Shack.

Near the diving area, Natalie, Jessica, and Bethany

stood facing Mason, Zach, and Tyler. They appeared to be in the middle of an argument.

Abby's breath quickened. Was Natalie confronting the boys with the evidence? Had Bethany found out about the spider plot?

"What's happening?" Abby asked eagerly, coming up beside them.

"We want to delay the diving contest." Zach cracked his knuckles. "For three days or so."

"So Mason can take diving lessons first?" Abby asked.

The girls snickered.

Zach's face reddened. "We just aren't, uh, ready in, uh, other ways."

"Did their spider collection escape?" Abby whispered to Jessica.

"Probably," Jessica whispered back.

"We don't want to delay," Bethany said. "We're ready to have the contest *now*."

"Why won't you change the date?" Mason demanded. "Just three little days, that's all we ask. Monday or Tuesday will be just as good."

"No!" Bethany cried. "Brianna is free on weekends only!"

"Come on!" Mason coaxed. "Who cares about

Brianna? You don't need her here when you lose the contest!"

"Yeah!" Zach and Tyler echoed. "Who needs Brianna?"

"For once, I agree with them," Natalie said under her breath.

Could Brianna dive as well as Bethany? Abby wondered. Even Brianna couldn't be the best at *everything*. Or could she? Bethany probably wanted to shine brighter than her best friend at least once in her life. And if Brianna saw her beat Mason, wouldn't she have new respect for Bethany?

Bethany folded her arms across her chest and scowled at Mason. "No Brianna, no contest."

Mason scowled back. "I won't do it tomorrow!"

"What about Sunday?" Jessica asked. "That's still the weekend."

"No!" Mason said.

"It's her best friend," Abby pleaded.

Bethany shot her a grateful look.

"Well, maybe," Mason conceded. "You're still going to lose, you know."

Bethany didn't reply. Instead, she adjusted her swim goggles, climbed the ladder of the diving board, and flipped backward into the pool.

Mason lumbered after her. He flopped off the diving board, belly first.

"See *that*?" Abby asked Zach and Tyler. "Or have you both gone blind from too many computer games?"

"The only way Mason can win is to cheat," Natalie announced.

"We're not cheaters!"

"Or wolves, either," Abby said.

"What???" Zach and Tyler glanced nervously at each other.

"We'd find out if you cheated," Jessica said smoothly. "Girls know these things. You can't hide anything from girls."

"Oh, sure," Tyler said. "Right."

Mason climbed out of the pool. "There's one thing we've forgotten," he said. "Who's going to judge the contest?"

"Us, of course," Abby answered. "Who else?"

"No way!" Mason pointed a wet, dripping finger at the girls. "That's three of you against Tyler and Zach! The girls outnumber the boys!"

"Who else then?" Natalie asked.

"We need someone fair," Jessica pointed out. "Who doesn't care who wins or loses."

Tyler said, "An outsider."

"My older sister Kathleen!" Mason snorted. "She'd love to see me lose!"

Abby nodded. "Good idea, Mason."

"I was *joking*!"

"One of my older sisters is on the swim team," Abby said. "The other one loves to give her opinion. Either of them could judge the contest, too."

Jessica gave Abby a quick hug. "That's the perfect solution!"

Their towels slung over their shoulders, Abby, Jessica, and Natalie approached the counter of the Snack Shack. Bethany was still at the diving board, practicing a while longer.

"A slice of pizza, please," Abby said, holding out a dollar bill.

"I'll have a small bag of popcorn," Jessica said. "And an orange soda."

"A hot dog for me," Natalie chimed in.

"I'm worried about what the boys are planning," Jessica said as the girls walked back to their chairs. "I think they have something more up their sleeves than spiders."

"Spiders up their sleeves! Ugh!" Abby cried.

"It's summer. They're not wearing shirts," Natalie pointed out.

"The boys have to hide the spiders *somewhere* if they don't have sleeves," Natalie continued. "Otherwise how do they get them on the diving board without attracting attention? Do they hold them in their hands? Hide them in their mouths?"

"*UGH!*"

"That's too disgusting even for Mason, Zach, and Tyler," Natalie mused. "I wonder what they're up to."

"Anyone want some pizza?" Abby offered.

"No, thanks." Natalie sat cross-legged on the grass and bit into her hot dog.

Jessica settled herself on a beach chair next to her. "Do you think they're still planning on using spiders to win?"

"Yes," Natalie said. "I . . ."

"Sssh! Here's Bethany!" Abby said. "We don't want to spook her!"

Bethany carried her goggles and a pair of flippers. She had a towel around her waist. It had pictures of gymnasts on it.

"Nice diving," Natalie complimented her. "And nice towel, too."

"Thanks," Bethany said. She turned to Abby. "How's Trouble today?"

"Trouble?" Jessica asked, raising her eyebrows. "There's lots of trouble around. Zach, Tyler, and Mason, to start."

"She means my kitten," Abby explained.

Jessica frowned. "You got a pet?"

"Uh-huh." Abby nodded.

"You didn't tell me!" Jessica cried.

"I've been busy taking care of him," Abby apologized. "I had to shop and clean and feed him. And I had to hide him from my family."

Her best friend didn't reply. She picked up her asthma inhaler and tossed it from one hand to another. Finally she spoke. "I can't believe you told Bethany and not me," she said.

"*Sorry*," Abby said. She should have told her best friend. But she hadn't. Instead, she had confided in Bethany during camp, and Bethany had given her lots of good advice.

"Pets are a lot of work," Bethany explained. "They can take up all your time."

"Tell us about your kitten," Natalie said eagerly.

"I got him from Heather. His name is Trouble, and he's gray with pale blue eyes," Abby began. "Every morning he jumps on me to wake me up. My parents are letting me keep him — for now, at least. . . ."

She broke off suddenly and slapped her forehead. "I forgot to feed him!"

"He'll be okay," Bethany said. "Did you feed him this morning?"

"Maybe. I don't remember." Abby jumped to her feet, gathered up her things, and threw her uneaten pizza into the trash.

She waved good-bye to her friends. They waved back, yelling encouragement as she sprinted toward the gate. All except Jessica.

Abby wished she could stop and explain things to her. Wouldn't she understand? After all, Jessica had been busy with her job for the last three weeks. When Abby had wanted to talk to her, she hadn't been around. It was easier to confide in Bethany — and anyway, Bethany was a pet expert.

But she had no time to talk about it now. Not to soothe Jessica's hurt feelings or to solve the spider problem. Abby couldn't leave Trouble alone and hungry in her room.

Chapter 12

Friday night

"If you want something done well, do it yourself."

Chalk and Blackboard Calendar

Or ask Isabel.

<u>Scene</u>:

A tired, hot, out-of-breath Abby Hayes rushes up the stairs to her room, expecting to find a starving kitten.

Instead, she finds a little gray kitten chewing contentedly on a toy mouse. Nearby, her older sister Isabel is sitting cross-legged on the floor. Her fingernails have been painted red, white, and blue. She is cooing at Trouble.

"You forgot to feed your kitten," Isabel

says in an icy voice. "This is no way to take care of a helpless animal."

One glance at Trouble's food dish confirms that Isabel has filled it with The Cat's Meow cat food. She has also given him fresh water.

"I heard Trouble meowing pitifully," Isabel continues. "The poor kitten's cries would have broken anyone's heart. I came in and fed him."

Abby hangs her head. Her SuperSib is right. "Thanks for taking care of him," she says in a low voice.

Isabel stands up and dusts off her shorts. She leaves Abby's room with a few well-chosen final words about responsibility.

As her sister leaves, Abby crouches down on the floor. She pets her kitten in a sad, remorseful way. How could she have forgotten this adorable kitten?

On the other hand, how could she desert her friends in their time of need?

"Ouch!" Abby said.

Trouble was in a frisky mood this Saturday morning. He had knocked a framed photo off the shelf.

He had jumped on Abby's head and meowed loudly to wake her up. Now he seemed to think that her sneakers were mice.

Just as she was tying her shoelace, he had pounced on her and accidentally scratched her hand.

"These are sneakers, Trouble," Abby explained. "You run in them, not after them."

His tail swishing, Trouble sat and watched as Abby crossed the room.

She glanced over at Trouble's water bowl. He still had water left. There was dry cat food in the bottom of his dish.

She was going to eat breakfast now. When she was done, she'd give Trouble the rest of the open can of The Cat's Meow cat food in the refrigerator.

"Don't make a big mess while I'm gone!" Abby warned.

"Meow!" Trouble answered.

Petting him one last time, she ran downstairs to the kitchen.

No one was there. Her mother and Eva had gone jogging together. Isabel was still asleep. Her father was up in his office. Alex was at his computer. Or maybe he was *in* his computer. Yesterday he taken it apart and put it back together again.

Abby got out the raspberry granola and sat down at the table. This morning, she'd have the comics all to herself.

PROCLAMATION! The words were written in red Magic Marker on a sheet of paper taped to the table.

THE HAYES FAMILY MUST COME TO A DECISION ABOUT THEIR VACATION SOON! SUNDAY NIGHT IS THE LAST NIGHT TO PRESENT YOUR CASE. IF THE FAMILY CAN'T AGREE, THEN MOM AND DAD WILL MAKE THE FINAL DECISION OR THE VACATION WILL BE CANCELED.

SIGNED,
PAUL AND OLIVIA HAYES

"Aaaaaah!" Abby cried, putting down her spoon.

She had promised to meet her friends at the pool this afternoon. She had to convince Jessica that they were still best friends. The girls had to stop the boys' plot before tomorrow. On top of all that, she had to come up with the final winning vacation plan!

Why did her parents have to be so fair? Why did they have to take everyone's opinions so seriously? There were so many of them! Why couldn't they just choose *hers*?

"Democracy can drive you crazy!" Abby muttered.

She grabbed her journal and began to write.

Living in the Hayes family is not easy!
My friends don't have the same problems I
do!

Natalie's parents make <u>all</u> the decisions
<u>all</u> the time.

"We never discuss vacations," she says.
"My parents let us know what we're going
to do and we have to act happy about
it."

(This would never happen in the Hayes
family. No one hides their thoughts and
feelings about <u>anything</u>.)

Jessica and her mom have only each
other to deal with. They take turns picking
vacations.

(If we rotated in the Hayes family, we'd
each choose a vacation every six years.
That means five out of six people would be
grumpy most of the time!)

I wonder what Bethany's family does.
Her little sisters are too young to complain
about vacations. Bethany's parents probably
listen to her.

(If I was the oldest, with three much
younger siblings, I'd always have my way!)

Abby closed her journal and glanced at the proclamation again. What was she going to do? What would Eva do? Or Isabel? Eva persisted in arguments until she wore the opposition down. Isabel used logic and facts. She always went to the library to research her projects. And look where it got her! She had won all kinds of awards and could out-argue anyone but their mother.

Abby quickly ate a few bites of cereal. If she went to the library now, she'd be back in time for the pool this afternoon. Then she'd patch things up with Jessica and figure out what the boys were going to do.

Taking her purple pen, she scrawled a note on the bottom of the proclamation. "Am biking to public library. Back before lunch. Abby."

"Do you want to look at books or magazines about popular vacation spots?" the librarian asked. "Or do you want to research the area where your grandmother lives?"

"My father already did that," Abby said. "I guess I can do it again. Maybe it'll give me new ideas."

"You can also go on the Internet," the librarian said. "However, we must have a signed permission slip from your parents. Do we have one on file?"

"I don't think so," Abby said. "We have the Internet at home."

She sat down at a desk with a pile of magazines and books and began skimming the pages.

There was a theme park near Grandma Emma's house. Alex might like it, although Isabel would hate it. There were historic canals that Isabel would like and Eva would hate. There were parks and a zoo and dozens of places that the Hayes family could visit, but . . . oh, forget it!

Abby groaned. Why did she even bother? Somebody was guaranteed to veto every idea she proposed.

Even though Dad was on Abby's side, they probably wouldn't win. Abby ought to just resign herself to going on a dumb, boring, stupid vacation.

It wasn't hard to give up the calendar factories. She'd always end up with new calendars, anyhow. It was Grandma Emma she didn't want to forget.

During one of the family discussions, her mother had pointed out that Abby had seen Grandma Emma less than six months ago.

"You mean *more* than five months ago!" Abby cried. She wished she could see her grandmother every month — or every week — or every day of the year.

No, she *couldn't* forget her favorite grandmother. There had to be a way to include her.

She glanced at the clock. If she went home now, she might write a letter to Grandma Emma, get ready to go to the pool, play with Trouble. . . .

"Oh, no!" Abby shouted.

Around her, people turned to stare.

"Is something wrong?" the librarian asked.

"I forgot something important," Abby mumbled, handing the magazines back to the librarian. She was embarrassed to have yelled in the library. Even five-year-olds knew better than that. "I have to go home right away."

"Come back with a signed permission slip from your parents, and I'll help you search the Internet," the librarian offered kindly.

"Thanks," Abby said, and rushed out of the library. Her face was burning. While she had been worrying about the family vacation, Trouble had slipped her mind *again*!

Chapter 13

But we have to do <u>some</u> things! Like take good care of our pets. I can't believe I forgot about Trouble again!

I don't even want to tell this to my journal. I accidentally shut Trouble in the closet. He purred and rubbed his head against my leg when I let him out. I felt <u>TERRIBLE</u>.

"I'm sorry, Trouble," I said. "I'll never do it again!"

Or will I? I've forgotten him twice in two days.

Is Trouble too much trouble for me?

Bethany takes care of her animals every

day. She's been doing it since she was five.

Maybe I'm just not used to caring for a pet. Maybe I need more time to get used to the responsibility.

But what if Trouble goes hungry while I'm getting used to feeding him or shut in a closet because I forgot he was there? Poor Trouble! It's not fair!

<u>Everything I'm Trying to Do</u>:
1. Take good care of Trouble
2. Come up with a vacation plan
3. Foil the boys' plot

<u>How Well I'm Doing Everything</u>:
1. Cat care: D-
2. Vacation plan: D+
3. Plot foiling: F (fortunately Jessica and Natalie are also on the case)

Oh, no! <u>I'm flunking summer vacation!!!!!!!!</u>

Abby closed her journal. She laid down her purple pen and leaned back in her chair.

With a loud meow, Trouble jumped into her lap. She scratched him behind his ears.

"I guess you forgive me, don't you?" she said remorsefully.

He purred loudly and settled into her lap.

As she stroked his soft fur, Abby studied the cat calendars on her wall. She wondered if Trouble looked at them when she was gone.

There was a knock on the door. "Can I come in?" Alex asked.

"You're allergic," Abby warned him.

Her little brother shrugged. "I don't care."

"Even if you start to wheeze?"

"Then I won't have to go out for fresh air and exercise." Alex ran his fingers through his hair so that it stood straight up. "Mom made me get off the computer," he explained.

"Too bad!" Abby sympathized.

"I'm going to Rollerblade. Will you come with me?"

Abby looked down at Trouble, sleeping peacefully in her lap. She didn't want to disturb him. On the other hand, she'd love to Rollerblade with Alex. She had promised him the day after the sleepover but had slept all day instead.

"Please, *please?*" Alex begged.

Then he began to sneeze.

"Okay." Abby pushed Trouble off her lap. In a moment, he was curled again up on her pillow. At least she wouldn't have to worry about him while she was gone.

When the ice-cream truck circled the park, Alex and Abby bladed over to it and bought ice-cream bars. Then they made their way to the nearest park bench.

"Did you eat lunch yet?" Abby asked as she unwrapped her ice-cream bar.

"No," Alex said, taking a large bite out of his.

Abby nibbled at the chocolate coating. "Me, neither."

The sun beat down on their heads. Abby glanced at her watch. It was almost one o'clock. "It's time to leave," she said. "I have to meet my friends at the pool in an hour."

"Can we skate around the fountain one more time?" Alex asked.

"Sure." Abby threw the ice-cream stick and wrapper in the trash, then stood up on her Rollerblades. "Race?"

"I'll beat you!" her brother cried out in challenge.

As they rounded the fountain, Abby was ahead. "I'm winning!" she yelled.

Suddenly, three dogs galloped straight toward her. She braked hard, lost her balance, and tumbled onto the grass.

Tails wagging, Elvis, Buddy, and Prince bounded over to greet her. They sniffed her Rollerblades and licked her hands and face.

"Whoa! Elvis! Buddy! Prince!" Jessica called. "Get over here! Now!"

Abby picked herself up from the grass.

"I'm sorry," Jessica said as she put the dogs back on the leash. She didn't look directly at Abby. "I shouldn't have let them run free!"

Abby examined the grass stains on her shorts and the dirt on her legs and arms. The pads had protected her knees, elbows, and the palms of her hands.

"I'm okay," she said.

Jessica didn't reply.

"Aachooo!" Alex sneezed as he petted Elvis. "Aaaaaacchhhooooo!"

Abby searched in her pockets for a tissue. "You're allergic to the entire animal kingdom, Alex."

"You'll be at the pool later?" Abby asked Jessica.

"Of course."

There was an awkward silence.

"Don't you understand?" Abby cried out suddenly. "Bethany's not my best friend! *You* are!"

Jessica flushed. "Am I?"

"Yes!" Abby took a few steps toward her friend. "I had to go to camp all by myself, without you. Bethany was the only person I knew." She took a breath. "I'm sorry I didn't call you and tell you about Trouble."

"You were busy," Jessica muttered.

"Yes, I was!" Abby retorted. "Trouble is a big responsibility."

Jessica didn't reply.

Abby turned to her brother. "Come on, Alex. Time to go home."

"Aaaaccccchhhhooooo!" Alex said.

"Wait!" Jessica took a breath. "You're right."

"I am?" She didn't expect Jessica to agree so quickly.

"I never thought about you going to camp by yourself," she admitted. "I was so jealous of Bethany."

"I like her," Abby explained. "But you're still my best friend."

"Really?"

"Truly. Honestly. Absolutely. Completely."

Jessica nodded. "I guess I was wrong."

"Next time I sneak a pet into the house, I'll call you right away," Abby promised.

Alex sneezed again.

"We should hug and make up," Abby said.

"We can't hug," Jessica replied. "We'd get all tangled up in dogs."

"And Rollerblades," Abby added. She looked down at her dirt-streaked legs. "I've had enough accidents for one day."

As she and Alex bladed home, Abby didn't notice the bumps and cracks in the pavement. She felt as if she were gliding on a smooth tarmac surface that went on for miles. She and Jessica were best friends again.

Not only that, but she had fed Trouble before she left. Now all she had to do was grab a bite of lunch, show up at the pool, and foil the boys' plot. Nothing to it! She was bound to succeed.

She and Alex removed their Rollerblades on the front steps. Then they went into the house.

As Abby ran up the stairs, her father was closing

her bedroom door behind him. Her heart began to pound.

"Is Trouble okay?" she cried.

"Trouble is fine." Paul Hayes sounded irritated. "But my office isn't. You left your bedroom door open, Abby. Trouble had an accident on my floor. . . . "

Chapter 14

Sunday

"Cheer up, the worst is
yet to come."

— *Philander Chase Johnson*

Optimist's Calendar

Oh, <u>no</u>! I thought the worst had already happened!

<u>Trouble's Worst</u> (so far):
1. Peed on Dad's office rug.
2. Jumped on Dad's desk and knocked files onto floor.
3. Dad's important papers fell onto wet spot on rug.

<u>Abby's Worst</u> (so far):
1. Had to go to store to buy rug cleaner out of my allowance.

2. Cleaned rug (ugh).

3. Spent two hours reprinting and filing Dad's papers.

4. Promised to keep Trouble in room and never let him out!

5. Too late to meet friends at pool. Friends still haven't figured out how to stop the boys. (Is this because I wasn't there?)

Is something worse than this going to happen today?

Today is the diving contest.

Today is also the day for the Hayes family to make their final decision about our vacation.

I am dreading today.

Abby's Memory Props:

Strings tied around fingers and toes: 20

Notes in pockets: 7

Reminders on calendars: 52

Abby's Checklist (To be used each time I leave house)

Trouble fed. (check)

Water dish filled. (check)
Trouble petted and played with. (check)
Trouble's litter box cleaned. (check)
Closet door left open. (check)
Door to bedroom firmly latched. (check)

On Sunday morning, Abby called Jessica on the phone.

"Today is D-day," she said. "D for diving. Are you as nervous as I am?"

"Yes," Jessica said. "Even though Bethany is doing the diving."

"I'm not worried about her — I'm worried about Zach, Tyler, and Mason!"

"Do you think Natalie should plant a tape recorder on them?"

Why do tape recorders get planted, Abby wondered. *They didn't look like seeds or even plants*.

"It's too late," she said. "The contest is only a few hours away. If we don't know now, we won't know at all."

"Mason, Zach, and Tyler better not do anything mean. If they do . . ." Jessica's voice trailed off.

"Bethany just *has* to win," Abby insisted. " 'Winning well is the best revenge.' " She had read that quote — or something like it — in one of her calendars.

"Yeah," Jessica agreed.

"Are you done?" her sister, Isabel, asked, coming into the room. She wore a long white skirt with a flowered halter top. "I have to make a call."

"Good-bye," Abby said to Jessica. She handed the phone to her older sister.

Isabel dialed a number. "Busy," she said, examining her fingernails, which she had painted in shades of orange, rose, and pink.

"Will you judge the diving contest?" Abby asked. She had asked her the night before, and Isabel had promised to think about it.

Isabel hit the redial button. "Eva can do it. She knows all about diving. I'm preparing my speech for tonight."

"Your speech?" Abby stared at her older sister. "You're giving a *speech* about our vacation?"

"Why not? It'll keep my debating skills fresh." Isabel put the phone to her ear. "I'd like to speak with Sophia, please."

Breathless, Abby sat down in a chair. Isabel was giving a speech. During the school year, her sister traveled around the country, winning debates. Did anyone in the Hayes family have a chance when Isabel decided to make a speech? Abby would have to resign herself to tattered Revolutionary War uniforms, rusty cannons, and empty battlefields. If she was lucky, she'd get a calendar out of it.

Bethany was upset. She kept looking at the clock next to the Snack Shack. "Where's Brianna?" she asked over and over. "She said she'd be here."

Everyone else was at the pool. The afternoon was hot and sunny, and both the large pool and the baby pool were crowded with swimmers.

Mason stood by the diving board in a pair of bright orange swim trunks. He kept glancing at Bethany. There was a rude smirk on his face. Nearby, Zach and Tyler whispered to each other.

"It'll all come out in the wash," Natalie said mysteriously.

"Wash? This is a swimming pool!" Abby said. *What was Natalie talking about?*

"Where is she?" Bethany repeated.

Jessica looked worried. "This isn't a good start," she muttered.

"Where *is* Brianna!" Bethany cried again.

"Here's Eva," Abby said.

Eva sauntered over to the girls. She was wearing a navy racing suit and had an umpire's whistle around her neck.

Abby felt a surge of pride. Her sister looked like a professional judge.

The other judge, Mason's sister, Kathleen, was flirting with the lifeguards.

"Ready?" Eva asked.

"Almost," Natalie said. "We're just waiting for — "

"Brianna!" Bethany cried.

On cue, Brianna entered the crowded pool area. She was wearing dark sunglasses and a blue bikini. Her sandals were leather. Her beach bag was woven straw. She nodded to the crowds of children as if they were an adoring audience.

"I had to rehearse a play," Brianna announced. "I have the starring role." She glanced at Natalie and then at Zach to see if they were listening.

"You said you'd be here half an hour ago." Bethany frowned at her best friend.

"The cast went out for ice cream. I couldn't say

no." With a sigh, Brianna put her bag on a chair. "I can't disappoint my fans."

"What about *me*?" Bethany asked.

Abby jumped in. "We're rooting for you, Bethany!" she cried. "Everyone is!"

"Go, Bethany!" Natalie and Jessica chorused.

"Go, Mason!" yelled Tyler and Zach a few feet away.

Natalie clapped her hands. "The great fifth-grade diving contest is about to begin! Will the contestants and judges please line up at the diving board?"

Bethany pulled on her swim cap. She fastened her goggles. "I'm ready!" she announced.

Mason slapped his arms against his chest. He took his place next to Bethany and then winked at Zach and Tyler.

"What . . . ?" Abby said.

"Have they gone back to kindergarten?" Jessica asked.

The boys were dancing up and down like demented five-year-olds.

"Are they out of their minds?" Brianna shrieked.

The boys stopped as suddenly as they had begun.

"Spiders!" they yelled. "Spiders! Near the diving board!"

Bethany froze. Her eyes widened. As her friends watched in horror, she backed slowly away from the diving board.

Chapter 15

Sunday   Still

"Look before you leap."

Frogs of Canada Calendar

Duck before you dive?

Bethany wasn't doing any of these things. She wasn't ducking or diving or looking or leaping.

She was standing still, not moving a muscle. Her body was rigid with fear.

Wrong!

1. Bethany didn't know there weren't any spiders. (Neither did we.)

2. She didn't know that the boys had made them up. (Neither did we.)

3. She didn't know that they were trying to scare her. (Neither did we.)

What she didn't know terrified and petrified her.

If she had known, she would have walked fearlessly to the diving board and executed the winning dive.

<u>What Happened Next</u>:
A lot of yelling.

Natalie: "It's a plot! They're making it up! Don't be afraid!"

I turned to Natalie: "<u>What</u> . . . ?"

Natalie hissed at me: "I'll explain everything later. Come on, we can't let Bethany lose!"

I took a breath and yelled to Bethany: "Listen to her! It's a spider-free zone! You're safe!"

Jessica: "Go on, Bethany! You can do it!"

Brianna: "Don't be chicken! <u>I'm</u> not afraid of anything!"

Zach, Tyler, Mason: "Spider! Spider! <u>Spider!</u>"

Eva and Kathleen: "Spiders! Where? What's going on? Is the contest canceled? We came out here for nothing!"

Bethany didn't hear any of it. She was too scared.

<u>What Happened Next</u>:

Jessica and I glanced at each other in despair. How could we restore Bethany's courage? How could we convince her that there was nothing to be afraid of? Was there _really_ nothing to be afraid of?

Jessica: "How do _you_ know the boys didn't let loose any spiders?"

Me: "That's what Natalie said. She promised to explain everything later."

We looked for Natalie. In the midst of all the excitement, she had disappeared. Suddenly, she reappeared at the side of the pool.

Natalie was wearing a long raincoat with a pipe sticking out of the pocket. In her right hand was a large magnifying glass. She had a Sherlock Holmes cap on her head, which was further adorned by a pair of furry ears.

"I'm Sherlock Hamster," she announced.

<u>What Happened Next</u>:

All were shocked into stunned silence.

"Hamster?" Bethany said. "Sherlock Hamster? You said _hamster_?" Her mouth twitched. Her nose wiggled. Suddenly, she burst out laughing.

Jessica grinned. I chuckled. And Eva gig-

gled. Brianna tittered. Kathleen shrieked.
Soon everyone was laughing. Even Zach
and Tyler. Even Mason!

Yes, Mason was laughing.

But not for long.

What Happened Next:

In her detective costume, Natalie crawled
on her stomach to the end of the diving
board, examining every inch of it with her
magnifying glass. Then she stood up, waved
the glass around, and announced in a ring-
ing voice, "I find no evidence of spiders."

What Happened Next:

The lifeguard blew her whistle and or-
dered Natalie off the diving board. "Swimmers only!" she said.

What Happened Next:

Bethany said, "I am going to dive!"

What Happened Next:

Mason turned pale.

<u>What Happened Next</u>:

Bethany climbed the ladder. Fearlessly, she executed a series of perfect dives. Everyone applauded, even Zach and Tyler.

Mason ran onto the diving board and belly flopped into the water. The judges unanimously declared Bethany the winner!

Yay, Bethany! Yay, Bethany! <u>Yay, Bethany!</u>

<u>What Happened Afterward</u>:

The girls rejoiced! Bethany won many exciting prizes! Among them were a Divers of the Deep Calendar, a cheat code for an electronic game, and a poster of the space shuttle. Eva gave her the umpire whistle she wore around her neck. Kathleen gave her a butterfly hair clip.

Zach and Tyler shook Bethany's hand. Brianna murmured about her first cousin, the Olympic diver. Mason said, "Good job," and burped loudly.

"Now let's swim!" Bethany said.
Brianna checked her watch. "I have to

go to my French lesson," she said. "_Au_
revoir, adieu, a bientôt. Ne m'oublie pas!"

"Nibble me what?" Natalie said.

"Don't forget me!" Brianna flipped
her hair over her shoulder. "I'm the
best!"

"Not at diving!" Jessica and Natalie
said together, throwing their arms around
Bethany. "Hooray for Bethany!"

Proclamation!!!! (My parents are not the
only ones who can do this!)

So many Hayes Book of World Records
were set today that they set a record of
their own!

Brianna wins for "Most Obnoxious Use of
French Language in a Public Pool Area."

Bethany wins for "Most Satisfying Victory
of Girls over Boys," as well as "Quickest
and Most Courageous Comeback in the History of the Fifth Grade."

Natalie wins for "Most Creative Foiling of
Evil Plot" and "The Sherlock Hamster
Award for Daring Detective Work" (also
known as the "Hammy").

Mason sweeps the "Bigger and Louder" category for belly flops and burps.

All three boys win for "Dopiest Dancing."

After we played Marco Polo in the pool for a couple of hours, Jessica and I treated Bethany and Natalie to ice cream.

"How did you figure out that there weren't really any spiders?" I asked Natalie as we sat on the grass with our ice-cream cones.

She smiled her mysterious smile. "I got Tyler to spill the spiders."

"He dumped out the jar . . . ?" Jessica said.

"Not really. It's just an expression. I mean, Tyler spilled the beans." Natalie paused to eat her ice cream, which was melting down the side of her cone.

"First spiders, now beans!" I said. "What are you talking about?"

"He told me all," Natalie explained. "He said that they decided against bringing real spiders into the pool area. He knew that just the mention of spiders was enough to terrify her."

Bethany flushed. "That traitor! I can't believe he said that!" she cried. "I'll never invite him over to my house again!"

"He was right, though," Jessica murmured.

Natalie nodded. "Abby told us how scared you were of spiders. I knew I had to distract you from your fear. So I got out my detective costume and added a pair of ears."

"It worked!" Bethany cried. "I laughed so hard at the Sherlock Hamster costume, I forgot to be afraid!"

"Natalie saved the day!" Jessica said. "And Bethany saved the dive!"

In fifteen minutes, I'm going home. Trouble will be waiting for me. (I hope no _real_ trouble is waiting for me!) It's not easy taking care of a kitten, especially when so much is going on. Like diving contests and family decisions. Tonight the Hayes family will decide on our vacation. Because of Trouble, I'm not well prepared. Will my day go from triumph to tears?

Chapter 16

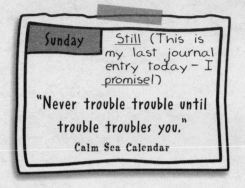

"**Never trouble trouble until trouble troubles you.**"
Calm Sea Calendar

Trouble has troubled me a <u>lot</u>. While I was at the swimming contest, he threw up on one of my favorite calendars, which was lying on the floor. Was he mad because I didn't spend enough time with him? I had to be with my friends at the pool!

"This is it!" I cried. I stamped my foot and burst into tears.

I didn't trouble Trouble, though. I cleaned up the mess (UGH!), gave him new food and water, and went to see Isabel in her room. She was making final changes to her vacation speech.

<u>What I Said to Isabel</u>:
"Please, please, please help me with Trouble! Trouble is too much trouble for me to take care of all by myself!"

<u>What Isabel Said to Me</u>:
"Sure, I'll help you out."

I threw my arms around her. "You're the best!" I cried.

"I have two conditions," Isabel warned.

"What are they?" I asked, with a sinking feeling. Knowing Isabel, she'd probably have me sign over my allowance for the next fifteen years.

"Number one, you vote for my vacation idea."

I hesitated for only one moment. What was a week of misery compared to years of cleaning kitty litter all by myself? "Sure, sis."

"Number two, you let me change his name."

"What's wrong with his name?" I demanded.

"I want to name him Jefferson! After Thomas Jefferson. It's much more distinguished than Trouble."

"That name is bigger than the kitten!" I protested.

"That's the deal — take it or leave it," Isabel said, folding her arms across her chest. One set of fingernails was painted a patriotic red, white, and blue; the other was Day-Glo green and orange.

"We've changed his name three times now. He's going to have an identity crisis," I pointed out.

"He'll adjust," Isabel said. "I'll take over half his care and he'll be in my room half the time. Trouble will have two people loving him, feeding him, and cleaning up his messes. What do you say?"

"If Mom and Dad let us keep him," I said, "the answer is yes."

"I'll work on them," Isabel promised.

Hooray! With Isabel on my side, victory is _almost_ certain!

What Happened at the Hayes Family Meeting Half an Hour Later (Leaving Out Fights, Arguments, and Disagreements):

I voted with Isabel and Alex, and our plan won 3-2-1. We are going to visit Williamsburg, Virginia, to see "history reenacted before our eyes." (A quote from Isabel's speech, which she gave, even though she knew she was going to win.)

We will also visit a nearby air and space museum.

Alex pumped his fist in the air. "We won! Yippee!"

"A trip to Williamsburg it is!" Mom said.

Even though she had lost, Mom was cheerful. "I love seeing democracy in action."

(What would she call my deal with Isabel? Desperation in action?)

"I guess I'll get lots of exercise going up

and down museum staircases," Eva said glumly. "Or wandering around old battle-fields."

Dad frowned. "Why did you go over to the other side, Abby? We still might have convinced them."

I hung my head. "I have my reasons, Dad," I mumbled.

I didn't feel bad about a week spent revisiting history. Mostly I felt terrible that Grandma Emma wasn't going to be with us.

Why wasn't she? Why couldn't she? If the girls could outwit the boys, couldn't I win over my family!

"We're not going to visit Grandma Emma," I cried, "but can't we invite her along?"

<u>What My Family Said:</u>
"Great idea, Abby!"
"Super!"
"Brilliant!"
(Why didn't they say this stuff to my other vacation ideas?)

Dad immediately picked up the phone and began dialing her number.

<u>What Grandma Emma Said:</u>

She said yes! She's coming to Williamsburg with us!!! It was that easy!

Happiness quotient for the Hayes family
has soared.

Not only will we see Grandma Emma,
but, as Mom and Dad pointed out, we
will also have more choices of what to do.
With three adults, we can split up and do
many different things. 3 adults over 7 days
means 21 choices. That means someone will
be happy all the time and everyone will be
happy some of the time.

Hooray! Hooray! <u>HOORAY!</u>

I get to spend a whole week with my
favorite grandmother PLUS my entire family
is grateful to me!

Will Mom and Dad let Isabel and me
keep Troub - Jefferson? Must ask while
everyone is hugging, kissing, and thanking me.

I'll promise to keep my room vacuumed so
that Alex doesn't sneeze too much and I'll
get Tr - Jefferson shampooed every month.

Can we take him on vacation, too?
Isabel will tell him all about his namesake,
Thomas Jefferson, who went to college in
Williamsburg. Maybe that will make him feel
better about his very long name.

Isabel just came into my room and
handed me $25.00.
"What's this for?" I demanded.
"Didn't you spend a lot of money on cat
food, toys, and litter box?" she asked.
"Well, yes, but . . ."
"This is my half." Isabel picked up
Troub — I mean Jefferson and cuddled him
in her arms. "I want to take him to my
room now. Okay?"
"Sure!" I said. (It's a lot easier to write
in my journal when Tro — Jefferson isn't
pouncing on my pen.)

Today has been a historic day. We figured out our family vacation. No one is
mad anymore! Everyone agrees. Isabel and
I are sharing T — Jefferson. Bethany beat
the boys!!

I feel like I'm "on a roll." Why on a roll? Why not on a breadstick? Or on a muffin? Or on a pizza?

(P.S. I still think Thomas Jefferson is a stupid name for a cat. I will call him T-Jeff for short!)